Protected

Also from Lexi Blake

ROMANTIC SUSPENSE

Masters And Mercenaries
The Dom Who Loved Me
The Men With The Golden Cuffs
A Dom Is Forever
On Her Master's Secret Service
Sanctum: A Masters and Mercenaries Novella
Love and Let Die
Unconditional: A Masters and Mercenaries Novella
Dungeon Royale
Dungeon Games: A Masters and Mercenaries Novella
A View to a Thrill
Cherished: A Masters and Mercenaries Novella
You Only Love Twice
Luscious: Masters and Mercenaries~Topped
Adored: A Masters and Mercenaries Novella
Master No
Just One Taste: Masters and Mercenaries~Topped 2
From Sanctum with Love
Devoted: A Masters and Mercenaries Novella
Dominance Never Dies
Submission is Not Enough
Master Bits & Mercenary Bites: The Secret Recipes of Top
Perfectly Paired: Masters and Mercenaries~Topped 3
For His Eyes Only
Arranged
Love Another Day
At Your Service: Masters and Mercenaries~Topped 4
Master Bits and Mercenary Bites~Girls Night
Nobody Does It Better
Close Cover
Protected

Masters and Mercenaries: The Forgotten
Memento Mori, Coming August 28, 2018

Lawless
Ruthless
Satisfaction
Revenge

Courting Justice
Order of Protection
Evidence of Desire, Coming January 8, 2019

Masters Of Ménage (by Shayla Black and Lexi Blake)
Their Virgin Captive
Their Virgin's Secret
Their Virgin Concubine
Their Virgin Princess
Their Virgin Hostage
Their Virgin Secretary
Their Virgin Mistress

The Perfect Gentlemen (by Shayla Black and Lexi Blake)
Scandal Never Sleeps
Seduction in Session
Big Easy Temptation
Smoke and Sin
At the Pleasure of the President, Coming Fall 2018

URBAN FANTASY

Thieves
Steal the Light
Steal the Day
Steal the Moon
Steal the Sun
Steal the Night
Ripper
Addict
Sleeper
Outcast, Coming 2018

LEXI BLAKE WRITING AS SOPHIE OAK

Small Town Siren
Siren in the City
Away From Me
Three to Ride
Siren Enslaved
Two to Love
Siren Beloved, Coming July 17, 2018
One to Keep, Coming August 7, 2018
Siren in Waiting, Coming Summer 2018

Protected

A Masters and Mercenaries Novella

By Lexi Blake

1001 Dark Nights

Protected
A Masters and Mercenaries Novella
By Lexi Blake

1001 Dark Nights

ISBN: 978-1-945920-99-8

Published by Evil Eye Concepts, Incorporated

Acknowledgments from the Author

As always I want to thank my whole team – Kim Guidroz, Danielle Sanchez, Stormy Pate, Riane Holt, Kori Smith, and my son who better have formatted this book properly! Thanks to Liz Berry and MJ Rose who built a place where authors can express themselves freely, can bring even their craziest ideas to life. This book really belongs in the Crossover Collection because Wade is the final bodyguard to find his happily ever after. I would like to thank my fellow authors – Larissa Ione, Carly Phillips, Corinne Michaels, J Kenner, and Susan Stoker – for bringing the bodyguards to vivid life.

Sign up for the 1001 Dark Nights Newsletter
and be entered to win a Tiffany Key necklace.

There's a contest every month!

Go to www.1001DarkNights.com to subscribe.

As a bonus, all subscribers will receive a free copy of
Discovery Bundle Three
Featuring stories by
Sidney Bristol, Darcy Burke, T. Gephart
Stacey Kennedy, Adriana Locke
JB Salsbury, and Erika Wilde

One Thousand and One Dark Nights

Once upon a time, in the future…

I was a student fascinated with stories and learning. I studied philosophy, poetry, history, the occult, and the art and science of love and magic. I had a vast library at my father's home and collected thousands of volumes of fantastic tales.

I learned all about ancient races and bygone times. About myths and legends and dreams of all people through the millennium. And the more I read the stronger my imagination grew until I discovered that I was able to travel into the stories... to actually become part of them.

I wish I could say that I listened to my teacher and respected my gift, as I ought to have. If I had, I would not be telling you this tale now.
But I was foolhardy and confused, showing off with bravery.

One afternoon, curious about the myth of the Arabian Nights, I traveled back to ancient Persia to see for myself if it was true that every day Shahryar (Persian: شهریار, "king") married a new virgin, and then sent yesterday's wife to be beheaded. It was written and I had read, that by the time he met Scheherazade, the vizier's daughter, he'd killed one thousand women.

Something went wrong with my efforts. I arrived in the midst of the story and somehow exchanged places with Scheherazade – a phenomena that had never occurred before and that still to this day, I cannot explain.

Now I am trapped in that ancient past. I have taken on Scheherazade's life and the only way I can protect myself and stay alive is to do what she did to protect herself and stay alive.

Every night the King calls for me and listens as I spin tales. And when the evening ends and dawn breaks, I stop at a point that leaves him breathless and yearning for more. And so the King spares my life for one more day, so that he might hear the rest of my dark tale.

As soon as I finish a story... I begin a new one... like the one that you, dear reader, have before you now.

Prologue

Broken Bend, TX
15 years before

Geneva Harris was going to die. It was right there and he was a horrible person because he kept her on the edge. That brilliant place only Wade Rycroft had ever taken her to was within reach, but every time she thought she would fall over the edge, he pulled his hand away.

"Not yet." He kissed her again.

She groaned. "It better be soon or my dad is going to be home and then you'll likely be facing the business end of that shotgun he never uses."

His gorgeous face split in a wide grin. Her heart threatened to seize because he was the single most beautiful guy in the world. The whole town was crazy for the Rycroft brothers, but not a one of them compared to hers. "Your daddy points a shotgun my way and I'll just marry you sooner. Now hush and give me what I want."

She'd been trying to do that for hours, it seemed. Wade kissed her again and moved over her, his gorgeous face staring down at hers.

She held on as he finally seemed to get serious. He thrust up and joined them together. This was where she always wanted to be, connected to the love of her life, holding on to him while he brought them pleasure.

He hit the right spot deep inside her and she went flying over the edge.

Of course she'd been flying ever since the day he'd kissed her six months before. She'd been tutoring him in geometry so he could graduate with his class. It wasn't because Wade wasn't smart. He simply hadn't been motivated. After a few weeks, she'd learned a lot about him and fallen madly in love. Everyone had been shocked when the nerd of Hamilton High School had started dating the senior class's most popular boy.

None more than her old friend Brock. She'd been fast friends with Brock Howard when they were young and her father had done some accounting work for his. Her dad had finally joined the Howard family company and they'd been thrown together a lot. He'd been an odd kid, the son of the wealthiest family in town, but none of the others ever seemed to want to play with him. He'd come back from private school the year before and he and Wade had hated each other on sight.

Wade fell forward and she welcomed his weight. In a matter of days, this feud between Wade and Brock would be over and they would be starting their lives. Wade was going to boot camp in the morning and she would spend the summer looking for a place to go to school. It would all depend on where he was stationed after his training, but she was going to make it work. If she had to get her degree online, then that was what she would do.

Her father was going to be disappointed, but she couldn't let that sway her. She loved Wade, and building a life with him was all that mattered.

He rolled off her but pulled her in close. "God, I'm going to miss this while I'm gone. Ten weeks. What was I thinking? I don't think I can be away from you for ten weeks."

She let her head rest on his chest. There was nothing she loved more than the sound of his heartbeat. "You're thinking we'll have a much better chance of eating and having a roof over our heads if you have a job. We can't stay here. Not unless you've changed your mind and you want to work on the ranch."

"There's no way. I can't stay here. I love my family, but I want more than to spend my life herding cattle and watching my back to make sure some rich shit doesn't stab me in it."

She winced but held on to him. She agreed with him about leaving but wished he would try to get along with everyone. He had a temper and sometimes it flared and struck out at the people around him. Especially Brock. "He's not that bad."

Wade sat up and she wished she hadn't said anything. "Maybe not around you. He plays nice around you, but there's something twisted about him. I wish you would stay away from him."

"My dad works for his mom. He's been their company accountant for years," she pointed out. "I can't exactly tell him I won't talk to him."

"You encourage him." He strode to her small bathroom, likely to dispose of the condom he'd used.

"What is that supposed to mean?" She held the sheet against her torso as she sat up in bed.

He strode back in, reaching for his boxers. "Baby, it means you're naïve and you don't see that massive ass for what he is." He leaned over and brushed his lips over hers. "And that won't matter because by the time summer is done, we'll be married and far out of the reach of Brock Howard and his wretched mother. Hell, if I'm being honest, it'll be good to be away from my family, too. I know things are tough and I can send some money back home. I love my mom, but that house…it's not the same since Dad died."

She reached out to him, taking his hand. His father had passed away a few months before of a sudden heart attack. All six Rycroft brothers and their mom were still reeling. "Are you sure you're ready to leave? Because we can stay here for a while. There's a community college I can go to."

He shook his head. "That's forty miles away. Absolutely not. You take this summer and have fun because in ten weeks you're going to be mine." He sat down on the edge of her bed, his hand on her hair. "I'll take care of you, Genny. You know that, right? We don't need a ton of money and we don't need this town."

Things would be lean. She would have to find a job, too, but that was nothing new. She'd started working her junior year of high school. Two jobs. She worked after school at the furniture factory Brock's parents owned, and she tutored junior high and high school kids. She wasn't afraid of hard work, and then they could send more money back to his mom. Her dad would be all right.

She nodded and wrapped her arms around him. "We only need each other."

"I wish you could come with me to the bus stop in the morning." He looked down at her wistfully.

"I can't make it." She would potentially lose her job, but she wanted to be with him.

He winced. "We need the money to buy a car. I wish…"

She wrapped her arms around him. "It's fine. This is our plan and we're going to make it work. The money I earn this summer will set us up."

He kissed the top of her head. "Damn, baby, I wish I could stay. I don't want to spend our last night apart. Ten weeks."

It sounded like forever, but she wasn't going to be anything less than optimistic. "The time will fly by. I promise, and you should spend tonight with your brothers. We have the rest of our lives."

"I love you."

She still couldn't imagine why he loved her, but she was happy he did. "I love you, too."

Two hours later, she'd showered and changed. Her father would be home soon and she was going to have to tell him she was leaving town and marrying Wade at the end of the summer. She wasn't taking the scholarship to UT Austin. She was choosing love.

He wasn't going to be happy about it. To mitigate his anger, she'd decided to make his favorite supper. It might get him in a better mood. After lemon pepper chicken and green beans with almonds, he would surely understand why she was dumping a scholarship in order to marry a soldier.

Her father had never liked Wade. She doubted some well-cooked poultry would change anything, but she had to try.

She took the stairs with a little hop in her step because it didn't matter. Her dad would be upset, but she knew what she wanted and she wanted Wade. She was eighteen years old and she got to make the decisions now.

She stopped in her tracks when she realized she wasn't alone in the house. Though it wasn't time for her father to come home, he sat in the living room. There was a grim look on his face, and he wasn't the only one. Emily Howard sat on the edge of the old brown sofa that had been in the living room since long before her mother had left them behind. The Howard matriarch perched there like she wanted to be able to move at the first possible moment. She was what Genny had heard called a "handsome" woman, with light blonde hair and a patrician face that would have been attractive if every feature didn't seem pinched with disdain. She sat next to Brock, who looked awfully self-satisfied.

And maybe Genny wouldn't be as scared if she'd merely come face to face with those three. Her father worked for the Howards. It wasn't so surprising they would be here.

But the fact that Alma Rycroft and her oldest son, Clint, were in the living room, too, was a shock to her system.

Brock stood. "Geneva, come and join us, sweetheart."

Was Wade right and she was being naïve about Brock? She was foolish. He'd only noticed her as anything more than a friend when she'd started dating Wade. "What's going on?"

Alma started crying and Clint held her hand.

"What's happened? Where's Wade?" Her heart threatened to beat out of her chest. Had something happened to Wade?

Clint stood. "Wade's fine, Genny. He's out with Heath and Clay. But we're here about Wade. I know you're planning on joining him when his training is done."

Her father looked up at her. "I was surprised to hear that."

"I was going to tell you," she said weakly. Okay, it wasn't the ideal way to tell him, but it was good to get it all out in the open. Why hadn't Wade come with them?

"Sit down," Mrs. Howard said. "It's time to explain how your future is going to work, dear. I'm afraid you won't be joining your little boyfriend after all. You have a life here in Broken Bend."

How had they found out? This was precisely why she hadn't told her father. "I think I'll make that decision on my own. If you'll excuse me."

When she turned to walk away, Brock blocked her path.

Genny felt a chill go down her spine and knew nothing would be the same again.

Chapter One

Wade Rycroft looked out over the yard where the reception was being held. It was still hard to believe that one of his brothers had finally taken the plunge. His oldest brother, Clint, had done the unthinkable and said I do.

What was even harder to believe was that Clint had invited Geneva Harris Howard to the festivities. Anger burned in his chest as he looked at the raven-haired beauty. Shouldn't greed show on that face of hers? How was it possible that she was even more beautiful than she'd been in high school? She should have gotten fat and ugly but no, she was curvy and gorgeous, and his dick still responded to her even when his brain knew she was toxic.

He took a deep breath and tried to let it go. He shouldn't let her ruin anything else in his life. On that night fifteen years ago, he'd sworn she had no power over him. Not anymore. She'd made her choice and she could live with it.

"I can't believe that harlot is here."

He wasn't the only one watching Geneva. The old biddies of Broken Bend were out in numbers, and they'd made their opinions of Geneva Howard plain. No one had sat with her. She'd taken a place at the back of the church on the bride's side. She'd been the only one in her row.

"Well, she's probably on the prowl, if you know what I mean," another said. "I heard she's desperate. The only asset the government didn't seize was the house, and Brock got that in the divorce."

"Brock got everything in the divorce. She signed a prenup. Even though she managed to lie and get poor Brock put in jail, the judge here wasn't fooled. It's those Austin types. They think they're so smart. They ruined this county."

"No, she did that. One of these days someone is going to give her what she deserves…"

Wade took a slow swallow from his longneck and glanced over at the tables set out on the lawn. They were a vivid white against the stark green of the grass. Damn, he hadn't realized how much he'd missed this place. The Rockin' R Ranch was where he'd grown up. He'd been born in the big house and spent his childhood running wild here. When he closed his eyes, he could still see his father on horseback, riding herd, and his momma ringing the bell that brought them all in for dinner.

Of course, he could also see Genny Harris, lying back on the grass by the pond, her eyes widening as he lowered his body to hers.

There was a reason he didn't come back often. Too many ghosts.

A hand clasped on his shoulder and he found himself smiling at his younger brothers. West and Rand were twins, both leanly muscled with all-American good looks and sandy blond hair.

He'd missed years with his brothers because of that woman, because he couldn't stand the thought of seeing her again. Even when he'd returned to Broken Bend, he would spend most of his time here trying to avoid Genny. That had been a stupid mistake.

It looked like karma was having its sweet way with her. It was definitely time to let go. It was time to forgive himself for being her fool. Maybe now he could relax and have a good time getting to know his brothers again.

"Clint looks good. I never thought she would get him in that tux," West said, tipping back his beer.

"You underestimate our new sister-in-law," Rand replied. "She's super sweet until you cross her, and then that girl can take a man down. When I complained about wearing a bow tie and asked her if I could maybe be a bit more casual, she told me I could wear the tie around my neck or she would find a new place to put it. I think she meant my balls. Now she didn't say she would wrap that bowtie around my balls, but she got that look. You know that look that lets a man know his balls are in trouble? Needless to say, I wore the tie in the traditional way."

West sighed as though he'd heard this all before. "You can take it off now. Your balls are safe."

Rand shrugged. "I want to be sure. When she's on a plane to

Hawaii, I'll take it off."

It was good to know there was a new matriarch of the Rycroft family. His mom had died ten years before and Clint had been left to keep the brothers in line. He'd been left to save the ranch.

Of course, that had become a hell of a lot easier when they'd found a rich natural gas reserve right beneath their feet a year and a half before. Another bit of karma. Genny had left him because she didn't want to be the wife of a poor soldier from an even poorer ranching family, and how those tables had turned.

Now the first family of Tellis County was in ruins, and the Rycrofts were enjoying more success than their daddy could have dreamed of. Clint had taken the initial money from the natural gas and brought the ranch into the 21st century. He'd joined a collective of independent ranchers, and the Rockin' R now supplied southern Texas with organic beef. Clint had been smart as hell.

Clint hadn't faltered because some girl dumped him.

"I'm sorry I wasn't here," he said, realizing how much he'd missed out on. "I'm sorry I let so many years go by."

West was staring at him like he'd grown two heads. "Sorry? You were serving your country, man. We're proud of you."

"I am in particular." Rand pulled at the hated tie but still didn't take it off. "Someone had to do it. There's been a Rycroft in the military for three generations. Momma used to say we produce too many damn boys. At least one of them had to be sacrificed to the US military. If only to feed him. I'm glad I didn't have to go. I don't think I would have been very good at it."

"I don't know," West said with a shake of his head. "You follow orders really well."

"Only if my balls are in question," Rand replied.

West sent him a look that had his brother snorting.

His youngest brothers had a shorthand of their own. Twins. He envied them. Sometimes he felt so solitary he ached with it. Especially now that all his friends were getting married and moving on with their lives. In the past couple of months, he'd watched the whole crew he worked with at McKay-Taggart Security fall for the women of their dreams and get married. A few of them had moved on, leaving him behind to start to rebuild his unit. Even his childhood friends were getting hitched, and now it looked like he would get to watch his brothers start their lives.

And he was still stuck. He looked out over the lawn again and she was sitting on her own, staring down at her phone. She hadn't eaten anything at the lovely plated dinner that had been served, and it looked like she wasn't going to partake of the open bar his brother had provided. He wondered if it wasn't lavish enough for her. He was certain the parties she'd gone to as Brock Howard's wife had been much more luxurious than a reception at a ranch.

Why the hell had she come? No one wanted her here.

"Who invited her?" The question was out of his mouth before he could think about it. Of course, if he'd thought about it at all, he wouldn't have asked. The last thing he wanted was for his brothers to think he was pining for a woman who'd dumped him years before.

Because he wasn't pining for her. It wasn't like he compared every woman to her and found them lacking. That would be stupid. He compared them to the woman he thought she'd been. He couldn't quite find anyone who moved him the way her lies had.

No, he was grateful to her. She'd saved him from his dumbass younger self.

West's jaw had gone stubbornly straight. "It sure as hell wasn't me."

"Hey, we talked about this." Rand sighed as though he knew he had to take the more mature role. "She's Lori's friend."

"Friend? I have no idea why Lori puts up with her." West had crossed his arms over his chest. "Clint has a soft spot for Genny. Always has. Even after she pulled that crap she pulled on you, Clint was right there. More than once I caught him in town having coffee with her over the years. He's the one who helped her move out of the mansion when they had to sell it because that husband of hers finally got what he deserved."

"Clint's not sleeping with her," Rand insisted.

Wade felt his gut twist at the thought of Clint and Genny together. How long had it been going on? Had she been cheating on him with more than one man? He wouldn't put it past her, but he'd thought better of his brother. "He spends time with her? And Lori lets him?"

"Of course she lets him because he's not sleeping with Genny." Rand was shaking his head. "Look, I don't begin to claim that I know what is going on between the two of them, but Genny's not a bad woman. I know she hurt you, Wade. But I think she's paid for that mistake. I feel bad for her, and I think Clint does, too. There are rumors I don't like to think about."

Rumors? When he'd left Broken Bend, he'd cut himself off from everything but news of his family. When Clint tried to relate some information that might have touched on Genny, he'd shut that shit down and fast. His big brother had learned not to mention her name if he wanted Wade to keep talking. He knew that the years he'd been gone, especially in the beginning, had been tough on Clint. Their mom died while Wade had been deployed. Clint had to keep everything together but if he'd sought comfort in Genny's arms, Wade wasn't sure he could ever forgive his brother.

Was he really thinking that way? It was obvious Clint loved his new bride, but Genny had a way of getting what she wanted.

"I'm glad you think so," West was saying. "I've never understood why Clint felt like he needed to help her out. You know he paid for her divorce attorney."

Wade's stomach took a deep dive. He looked out over the lawn, the twinkle lights coming on as the band began to play. Clint escorted his bride out to the floor for their first dance as man and wife.

Genny still sat by herself, her face tight and drawn as she looked out over the dance floor. Was she pissed off that she might lose her sugar daddy? Or was she planning on how to catch another wealthy husband? There were a couple of men at this wedding who could keep her in lavish style. Jack Barnes, the man who owned the successful ranching collective his brother had joined, was sitting with his wife, Abby, and his partner, Sam Fleetwood. Barnes was a highly connected businessman and rancher who could introduce her to any number of rich men. He was sure she would prefer to be married to one of them, but she wasn't eighteen anymore and she came with the encumbrance of a kid. There were men who wouldn't want to raise Brock Howard the fourth. She might have to settle for being some rich man's mistress.

But she wasn't going to be his brother's mistress. No fucking way.

"Wade?"

He wasn't sure which brother called out his name. All he knew was it was time to break his silence with her. He'd tried to avoid her, but now he realized he couldn't. He wasn't going to allow her to ruin his brother's life.

She glanced up, her eyes widening when she realized he was coming her way. She stood, straightening the dress that was a bit too loose on her. Now that he was closer to her, he could see the fine lines around her eyes. It was good to know time hadn't left her completely unmarked.

"Wade, I was hoping we could talk." Her voice was huskier than he remembered. "Could we go somewhere quiet?"

Was she seriously trying to get him alone? Did she think she could turn those big blue eyes on him and he would forget about everything she'd done?

He was well aware that stares were turning his way, but he didn't care. He wasn't going to cause a major scene, merely let her know the rules. It was obvious something was going on between her and his oldest brother. That stopped here and now.

"We don't need to go someplace quiet. We can do this right here and right now. I understand that you've been spending some time with Clint. I don't care what you do with other men. God knows how many you've run through by now, but you need to understand I won't allow you to break up my brother's marriage. How much to get you to leave town and not come back?"

He had some money saved up. When they'd found the gas reserves, he'd been given his cut. He didn't live lavishly so he had a sizable amount collected in his account. He hated the thought of spending it on her, but if it saved his brother, he would do it. And when Clint got back from his honeymoon, they would have a long talk.

She'd paled visibly. "How much?"

"Money, sweetheart." The word came out twisted and nasty. "I'm asking how much it will take to get you to stay away from my brother."

"Wade, you have the wrong impression."

He wasn't going to give her a chance to work her magic. She was smart and she'd always known how to manipulate him. "I don't think so. How much have you already gotten out of him? I understand he paid for your divorce lawyer. What happened? Did you not love your husband as much when he lost his fortune? Why didn't you sell some of those fancy clothes of yours and pay for your own damn lawyer?"

Her eyes were steady on him. "I'm paying Clint back."

"I'm sure you are. My question is what are you paying him back with?" He was well aware of the nasty insinuation.

"I didn't come here to fight with you," she said, her voice a bit tremulous now. "Please, Wade. I know you're angry with me, but I need to talk to you. There are some things you don't understand."

"We have nothing at all to talk about except for you to give me a number," he shot back. "If you don't give me that number and then get your ass out of town, I'm going to do what I should have done all those years ago."

Tears shone in her eyes, but her face had gone stubborn in a way he'd never seen before. "And what is that? What should you have done all those years ago?"

He leaned in, well aware that he was getting in her space. He prided himself on being a gentleman, but she brought out the asshole in him. "I should have crushed you. I should have made your life hell. I'll do it this time. By the time I'm finished with you, you'll wish you'd left town. You'll wish you'd taken that brat of yours with you."

A loud smack split the air around him and it took a second for the pain to hit. She'd slapped him good. His face heated. Had he really just threatened her kid? Who the hell was he? He didn't recognize himself.

Still, he couldn't take it back.

"What the hell is going on?" Clint stepped up, looking resplendent in his tux. He held hands with his bride.

"Hey, are you all right?" Lori wasn't talking to him. She moved to Genny's side, placing a hand on her shoulder.

He didn't understand a thing. Maybe there was something more going on here. "I think she's fine. I'm sure she's heard worse. And maybe I was hasty. Maybe Clint knows exactly what he's doing."

"What the hell is that supposed to mean?" Clint asked.

He held his hands up, backing away. This was his big brother. Clint had taken care of them all. After their dad had died, it had been Clint who stepped in, giving up his chance to go to college because he had to run the ranch. And yet all Wade could see at the moment was his big brother in bed with Genny, enjoying her every curve and that sweet as sin mouth of hers. "It means your sex life and what your wife is willing to put up with is absolutely none of my business."

Clint's face went red and Wade realized no one was dancing. They were all far too busy watching the family drama playing out in front of them.

Lori had blushed as well, but she simply smiled and waved toward the band and dance floor, nodding. The band changed songs, starting up a beat perfect for the latest line dance. "Please, dance. Have fun! This is nothing but a small misunderstanding between brothers."

Abby Barnes dragged her husbands, Jack and Sam, out on the dance floor and the rest of the group joined in.

Clint turned to him, his voice going low. "You want to explain to me why you've decided to wreck my wedding? And I would love to know exactly what you're accusing me of."

Heath Rycroft made his way through the crowd. "What's going on?"

"I'd like to know that myself," Clay said.

West and Rand joined the circle. The gang was all here.

And it was obvious that he was the one left out. They were all looking at him like he was some kind of freak, like he was the troublemaker. Well, he'd walked out on them. He hadn't come back because he couldn't stand the thought of seeing her again. The years and distance had turned him into an outcast. Genny had won and she would continue to win. Lori held her hand and his new sister-in-law frowned his way. It was definitely time to retreat. His brothers didn't need him.

Anger boiled inside him. "It was a mistake to come here. Lori, I'm sorry I ruined your reception. Clint, I thought I was saving you, but you have obviously made your choice. Hope you have fun with her."

"We need to talk." Clint took a step toward him.

He held his hands up because he was done talking. "No. We don't. I need to go back to Dallas and you need to get on with whatever it is you're doing. Y'all have a nice night."

"Don't be an asshole," one of his brothers said. He couldn't tell which. There were a lot of them. Three older, two younger. He was somewhere in the middle and the truth was they hadn't missed him. They had each other.

And apparently at least one of them had Genny.

He stalked off, tearing at the tie at his throat. It had been a stupid idea to come home after all these years. There was absolutely nothing left for him here. He would head back to Dallas and the life he'd built there. If he hurried he could make it into work in the morning. He'd taken the week off, but the thought of sitting in his quiet house with nothing to distract him was unsettling. He needed work, the harder the better. He would ask Tag to send him on the worst assignment possible, one where taking a bullet was almost certain. Then he could spend his time surviving and not thinking about Genny Harris.

Howard. She'd made that choice. It didn't matter that she'd divorced the bastard. She would always be a Howard to him.

As quickly as he could, he made his way to the house and picked up his duffel. He hadn't exactly unpacked. The truth was he'd tried to spend as little time in his room as he could. Ghosts. They were everywhere in this house, but particularly strong in the room he'd grown up in. Someone had thought it was a good idea to make it a shrine to his teenaged years. It was exactly as he'd left it. The desk where he'd done his homework was still pushed against the wall and the buckles he'd won during his rodeo days were on display.

And there wasn't an inch of this room she hadn't imprinted herself on. He'd made love to her on the bed, sneaking back in when everyone else was at a church dinner. He'd lied to his parents about having to study for a test and then he'd been the tutor. Most of the time she knew way more than he did, but when it came to sex, he'd been the teacher. He'd lost his virginity at sixteen to a barrel racer, but it hadn't been until Genny that he'd finally realized what sex could mean.

And it hadn't been until Genny that he'd realized how stupid he was. She kept teaching him that lesson even fifteen years later.

He slung the duffel over his shoulder and started down the stairs. He wasn't coming back here. Dallas was home now.

He'd made it to the bottom of the stairs and turned to go when he realized he wasn't alone in the big ranch house.

"All right, you son of a bitch, we'll do this the hard way."

He saw her through the mirror in front of him. She was standing there like a warrior, her eyes wild, and she hadn't come unarmed. Yep, she'd pulled a gun on him. It looked like Genny wasn't done with the lesson for the day.

Chapter Two

Genny held the pistol in both hands, her feet planted firmly. Clint and Lori had gone over and over how to handle her recently purchased firearm. Of course, she was certain at the time, they hadn't thought she would be holding it on their kin.

But damn it, he'd pushed her too far.

She'd promised Ash she wouldn't do anything crazy. Actually she'd specifically promised her son that she wouldn't point a gun at her high school boyfriend. One more promise she'd broken.

At least she could tell him she'd kept the safety on, and after Wade's complete assholery, that was a true sign of her maturity.

He held his hands up. "Can I turn around or do you plan on shooting me in the back? Last time you used a knife."

Yup, she wished she hadn't promised her only child she wouldn't commit murder tonight. "You can turn around."

Slowly he turned, and then she wished she'd kept him facing away from her. He was almost too beautiful to look at. Pitch black hair and soulful brown eyes. The man was even more overwhelming than the boy she'd known. He'd put on muscle and seemed to be taller than he'd been, but that might be a trick of her memory. Or it might be because in the years that spread between them, she'd been made so small.

He'd gotten more handsome, more masculine, and she'd been reduced to nothing. Sometimes she felt like she'd died that day and only came back to life for brief periods. She was a walking shell and always would be if she didn't take control of this. This was her one and only chance. Perhaps she could have avoided this scene if it had only been *her* chance, but it was Ash's only chance, too, and that meant everything to her.

"You owe me, Wade Rycroft." She'd been waiting fifteen years to say those words. "And the time has come to pay up."

"I owe you?"

"Yes. You owe me and I've come to collect. Here's how this is going to go," she started.

Before she could begin to explain her plan, he was on her. His left hand chopped up, batting her hands and making her lose her grip on the pistol. It clattered to the floor, banging against the hardwoods. He gripped her wrist, dragging it around her back as he shoved her against the wall.

She found herself caught as he pressed himself in, using his weight to hold her still.

"You think I owe you? I see things differently, darlin'." The words were spoken softly against her ear. He was close enough that she could feel the heat of his breath, but there was no way to mistake the words coming from his mouth as anything but cold. "I think you owe me."

Her breath hitched and she struggled against him. Rage formed in her gut. Or maybe it was always there and he simply turned the furnace up a notch. "Let me go, you bastard."

He pressed in and suddenly she could feel something hard against her ass. "Not until I figure out exactly why you decided to pull a gun on me. Did you think I'd let you get away with that? Damn it, Genny. Stop squirming. Please."

The *please* coming out of his mouth sounded so much like her Wade that she went still for a moment. "Let me go."

"Could I have a minute? I need to calm down. I don't want to hurt you. Stop fighting me and don't pretend you're the victim here. You pulled the gun on me. And I'm sorry about the…I'm sorry about that. Adrenaline can do that to a man. I don't want you to think I'm going to hurt you."

She closed her eyes to try to keep the tears from flowing. God, even when she'd pulled a gun on the man he was concerned for her. He would rip her heart out, but he wouldn't hurt her physically. Unlike her ex-husband.

She'd made the right decision.

"The safety was on." Maybe that would get him to back off. She needed to bring the tension in the room down.

"It doesn't matter. You threatened me and I'm not about to let that pass. I know I've been your fool before, Genny, but I'm a different man now." He'd calmed considerably, but there was still anger in his tone.

"You weren't a man at all. You were a boy who got hurt and never looked back." Despite the violence that marked the beginning of this encounter, there was a piercing sweetness to feeling his warmth, breathing in his familiar scent. Even after fifteen years she could remember that woodsy, masculine scent that was uniquely Wade. It reminded her of the last time she'd felt safe.

It was all a lie, of course. But he still owed her. She wasn't coming to him for love or even pleasure. She only wanted protection. When her son was safe again, she would walk away and they would finally be done.

"Hurt? You think what you did hurt me?" He pushed away from her and she could breathe again. "You did me a favor. I'm sorry I never thanked you for it. Getting married to you would have been the worst mistake of my life. I was a dumb kid and you saved me from myself."

Damn that hurt. She'd gone over and over this meeting in her head for days and she'd thought she'd been prepared for his anger. His disdain. God knew she'd gotten used to disdain over the years. Brock had twisted her reputation when he'd needed to. He'd made people she'd known all her life hate her. But somehow knowing Wade hated her hurt worse.

He picked up her gun, shaking his head. "I'll keep this. Now, I'm going to talk to the sheriff. I think I saw him on the dance floor. You'll enjoy prison. Maybe they can reunite you with your dear husband."

"Give it back to me." She might have lost her chance to talk with him. He wouldn't even give her the time of day, but she couldn't be without the gun.

Cool brown eyes rolled as though she'd said the stupidest thing possible. "No. I might be willing to forgo sending you to jail though. Let's talk about you leaving my brother alone."

She didn't really hear anything past the word no. She'd spent everything she had left on that gun. Brock would be out of jail soon. He would come straight for her.

I promise you, I'll make you wish you'd never been born. And then I'll take my boy back.

He couldn't leave with her gun. Panic threatened to overwhelm her.

"Give me my gun." The words came out surprisingly calm given the fact that she could feel her heart pounding. Her time was running out and Wade wasn't going to help her. She could likely tell him what she'd done all those years ago, how idiotic she'd been, and he would laugh. He might not be as violent as Brock, but he was a man. She'd made him look foolish. It wouldn't matter that she'd done it for the best reason possible. Men only cared about their own egos. If a woman threatened that, she would get ground under his boot.

Which was precisely why she needed that gun.

"No," he replied implacably. "Now are we having a talk with the sheriff or are you going to pack your bags and get the hell out of town? No one wants you here. I have no idea what the hell you've done because I didn't care enough to ask about you, but if there's one thing I've figured out, it's that these people hate you. You might have tricked my new sister-in-law into a friendship, but that's over now. You've done enough to this family."

Enough. She'd done enough? She'd lost everything and now he wanted to take more. All the years of pain and abuse came rushing back and suddenly she didn't really see Wade in front of her. She saw Brock. She saw his mother and her father. She saw everything and everyone who had conspired to wreck her life and yes, he was in there, too. He'd been the reason she'd walked through Hell.

One minute she was standing in front of him and the next, she attacked. Her vision had bled to red and she felt her fists pounding against him, nails trying to scratch him. She went wild, everything she'd shut down coming out again now that she was in the room with the man who'd started it all. All the pain and humiliation. All the aching years of loneliness. He wasn't taking another single thing from her.

"Goddamn it, Genny," he was yelling as his arms came up to ward off her attack. He stumbled backward, falling on his ass.

She was on him in a second, but he was too good, too strong. He caught her hands and flipped her over and once more he held her down with his bigger, stronger body.

Story of her life. She was weak. She was powerless. She couldn't even protect her son.

"Genny, why do I owe you?" There was a scratch on his face that welled with blood, but his eyes were wide and he looked down on her with something like concern. "What's going on?"

"Get off me."

He shook his head. "No. Not until you tell me why I owe you. What do I owe you? No woman goes that crazy unless something terrible happened to her. What am I missing?"

Perversely, she couldn't tell him now. She had to get him off her. She tried to bring her knee up, tried to get at the part of him that was hard and male, but he was too close.

"Hush, baby." His voice soothed, hands gentle on her now. "Genny, calm down. It's all right. I need to know. Tell me what I owe you."

"Everything," a familiar voice said. "You…we owe her everything, brother. And it's time you heard the truth."

She blinked back tears because Clint was here and she would finally have to tell her tale.

* * * *

Wade stared at her across the living room, his whole soul aching. He had no idea what she'd been through, but it had been bad. His gut twisted into a knot. What the hell had happened to her?

You owe me.

She'd looked haunted when she'd said the words and damn it, she'd been holding a gun. When he'd known Genny Harris, she'd been the single gentlest soul he'd ever met. She believed in talking out her problems, in the good of all stinking mankind. She'd been naïve but in the best way possible. She hadn't been the kind of woman who drew down on a man.

And god, he wasn't even sure how to describe that moment when she'd flown across the room, rage and fear in her eyes. He'd been around enough PTSD to know it when he saw it.

She'd made a terrible choice, but it looked like she'd paid far more than he could have guessed, and it was time to stop being angry with her. She'd been his first love. She'd given him her virginity and spent endless hours knocking math into his head so he could graduate.

He did owe her. He owed the dumbass kids they'd been.

"Let me get you a blanket," he said.

She didn't look up. "I'm not cold."

He could easily see that wasn't true. "Baby, you're shaking."

"Don't call me that. I'm not your baby." She turned to Clint, who was walking back into the room, a bottle of Scotch and three glasses in his hand. He'd taken off his tuxedo jacket and chucked his tie. "Clint, I should go. I need to get back to Asher. I'm going to call someone to pick me up."

Why did she need someone to pick her up? She hadn't had much to drink.

Clint frowned her way. "You're not going anywhere. You wanted to talk to him for a reason. That reason hasn't changed."

"No, but he has," she replied.

He hated the fact that it felt like they were having a whole conversation he didn't understand. But the truth was he'd acted like a complete jackass and he was starting to think he would regret it if he kept it up.

Clint shook his head as he poured out the Scotch. "He hasn't. Not really. After all these years, he's still jealous and that's what making him behave atrociously."

He would only take it so far. "I'm not jealous."

His brother passed him a glass after handing one to Genny. "Sure you aren't."

"I'm not," he insisted. "I got over this a very long time ago." Probably a lie but he couldn't admit the truth. She'd walked out on him. He wasn't the bad guy here. She'd chosen money and power and a nice house over love. Maybe it was time to truly put the past in the past. He could be civil to her. It seemed she'd suffered a lot. He could feel pity for her. What he wouldn't allow himself to feel was attraction. Not that his dick was listening. His dick had nearly jumped off his body the minute he'd gotten close to her. "I'm sorry if I offended you tonight. I apologize. Now, could you explain what you need from me?"

"I don't need anything from you," she replied, her eyes on the glass in her hands. She took a sip and then another. And then drained it dry.

So she'd taken to drinking. Maybe she did need a ride home. It wasn't terribly surprising. Living with that asshole Brock had to make a woman crazy.

"She does need something from you. Something I can't provide," Clint replied.

"My question is why are you providing her with anything at all?" He couldn't seem to help himself. Why couldn't he watch his damn words around her?

"But you're not jealous," Clint remarked with a deadpan huff. "Genny, he's still who he was all those years ago and he owes you."

She stood up, her face pale. "I've changed my mind. I don't want to do this. I'll find another way."

Clint turned to him. "Fifteen years ago the Howard family bought the loan on our ranch and immediately called it in. Brock Howard came out to the house the day before you left for boot camp and explained that if we didn't come up with fifty thousand, he would foreclose."

"What?" He'd never heard a word of that. As far as he'd known they'd never had real trouble. He'd known the ranch hadn't paid well until the year before, but he hadn't heard a damn thing about them almost losing it.

Genny had sat back down, her spine straight as she stared out the window at the party still going on. Her face was set in mulish lines as though she was angry Clint was talking.

Why would she be angry? She wouldn't have had anything to do with a foreclosure. Her father had been an accountant, but he'd worked for the Howard family's private business. Maybe he'd advised them, but that wouldn't have been Genny's fault. The only thing that connected Genny to a possible foreclosure would be the fact that Brock Howard had been obsessed with her and she'd made the decision to…

The truth hit him squarely in the gut and reframed the past fifteen years in a way that made him sick. He was the one downing the Scotch now. He swallowed it. All of it. With shaky hands, he poured himself another. "Brock didn't want the money. He wanted Genny. He traded the ranch for Genny."

"Yes." With one word Clint affirmed his fear. "He told our mother if you walked away with Genny, he would foreclose and see everyone out of our home."

"And Mom let it happen." He stood. He couldn't sit. His skin felt too tight. What had she done? His mother had put this on the slender shoulders of an eighteen-year-old girl? "She went to Genny? She asked her to do this?"

The world felt like it was spinning, and he was quite certain he wouldn't be happy where it stopped.

"Don't blame her," Genny said, the words dull coming from her mouth. "She'd recently lost her husband. Your mom was left with six boys to provide for, and the ranch was in bad shape at the time. What was she supposed to do?"

"Dad was stubborn. He wouldn't change, just kept raging at the machine," Clint said. "When he died, the ranch was damn near bankrupt, but it was all we had. Honestly, I thought if we just had a year or two we could turn it around. I pushed Dad to look into organic cattle. He wanted to keep going the way we had, but we couldn't compete with corporate ranches or bigger ones."

Outrage pierced through him. "That wasn't her responsibility." His anger had shifted from Genny to his mom and oldest brother. How could they have done this? How could they have put this on her? They'd lied to him. "I got a Dear John letter from Genny. Did you tell her what to say to get me angry? Now that I think about it, that letter was completely out of character. Did you write it for her?"

"What were they supposed to do, Wade?" She looked beyond tired, her voice low. "Was she supposed to give up her home and make her sons live on the streets for your high school crush?"

How could she say that? "Don't make this less than it was. I loved you. I was ready to marry you."

Her eyes stared through him. "And when I wrote you a letter that was completely out of character, that ran utterly counter to everything you knew about me, what did you do? Did you call me to find out what was going on? Did you rush home to work it out? Or did you take the first chance you had to get out of our relationship?"

He stopped, not wanting to think about what she was saying. His life had ended that day. Or at least it had felt that way at the time. "That's not true. I was sick to death for months after that damn letter. I did call home. I called and talked to Clint when I could use the phone. Of course, Clint told me all about the wedding you were planning. I didn't come home after that."

"Fifteen years, Wade. You say you loved me but the first time I made you angry, you left and didn't come back for fifteen years. You say I was the woman you loved, but you didn't even try to call me. You called Clint and told your brother I'd saved you from making a terrible mistake and moved on with your life, and do you know what I did? I married Brock anyway. I saved your family anyway because that was how much I loved you."

He had to take a deep breath because he felt sick. He couldn't be sick. It was weakness and it appeared he'd been weak enough. "I lied. I didn't want Clint to see how much I was hurting, but I…" What could he say? He hadn't gone after her. He'd been in the middle of boot camp. He'd chosen to stay in South Carolina. Even when he'd had the chance to go home, he'd spent that first free weekend with his buddies getting drunk and chasing skirts.

It had been the first time he'd been with another woman after Genny. He'd been faithful the whole time they'd been together. He'd forced himself to do it, told himself she was having a grand old time with her fiancé.

"What did Brock do to you?" He asked the question, but he wasn't sure he wanted to know. What had been happening to her while he'd been drinking and fucking and cursing her name? He turned to his brother, emotion making him twist and turn. "How could you not tell me?"

"I made him promise he wouldn't." Her shoulders had relaxed, and she took a step toward him, her hand coming out before she stopped. She kept the distance between them. "I thought I knew what I was doing. And Wade, you didn't really want me. Like I said, if you loved me, you would have done something, anything. You wouldn't have sat back and let it happen. I know you. At least I knew the you back then. You were a fighter. I waited my whole wedding day. I knew you would show up and I would have to find a way to stop you from stopping me. I had it all planned out, but you didn't show. You didn't come for me."

He *was* the villain in the piece. "I was angry with you."

"Wade, she needs your help," his brother said.

"Get out." He couldn't stand to look at Clint right now.

"Hey," Clint began.

He shook his head. "No. You go. Maybe in a couple of years I'll be able to forgive you but damn straight not on the day when you're marrying your dream woman and you're the reason I lost mine."

Clint looked ashen. "What was I supposed to do?"

"You were supposed to tell me," Wade shot back. "You were supposed to give me a chance to figure it out. You were not supposed to put an innocent girl through hell. She wasn't yours to use. Damn it. Even if she hadn't been mine, she wasn't yours."

"And what would you have done?" Clint asked. "Would you have let your momma get kicked to the curb?"

"It wasn't Genny's responsibility. So yes. If that was the choice, yes,

I would have made it. We had relatives who would have taken us in. We had choices, and you took hers away. Tell me, brother, tell me if you would have done the same thing to Lori. Tell me if you would have sent her to be raped by another man to save your fucking ranch." He couldn't breathe in here. He looked to Genny and did what he should have done a long time before. He took control. "Get your things. We're leaving. We can talk about what you need from me on our way to your son."

He held his hand out and was shocked to see it shaking. But he wouldn't pull it back. He'd failed her once and it had cost them years. He wouldn't make the same mistake again. The minute he'd realized she hadn't betrayed him, something deep inside him had opened, a place he hadn't felt in fifteen years. Some spark he'd lost shot back to life again.

He'd never stopped wanting her. Maybe he didn't deserve her after what his family had done, but he couldn't walk away. Between the divorce and her…he couldn't think of that man as her husband…Brock going to jail, she'd lost everything. The factory had closed, and it appeared she didn't even have the money for a car.

Another thing he laid at his brother's feet.

What would he do if she wouldn't come with him?

She stood and stared at his outstretched hand for one long moment. If she walked out, he would follow her. He wouldn't force her to come with him, but he would watch over her. He would figure out what her problem was and try to find a way to solve it for her. He would find out where she lived and anonymously send her the things she needed to be comfortable.

She and her son. God, she had a son. She'd had Brock's son.

Her hand came out and covered his. "It's okay, Wade."

A flash of their past together burned through him.

It's okay, Wade. It's all going to be okay. I'll be with you for everything. We'll get through the funeral and we'll go from there. Hold on to me.

He saw her through watery eyes. "It's not okay. Tell me what you need."

When he threaded their fingers together, she didn't pull away. "I need a ride back to my place. I can explain it to you on the way."

Her hand was in his and that seemed to quell the rage that had threatened to burst forth. He was able to somewhat calmly look to his brother. "Who else knew? Besides you and Momma? The twins didn't seem to understand why you spent so much time with her."

"Besides my wife, Clay is the only one who knows," Clint replied. "I didn't tell Heath or the twins. They didn't need to know how close we came to losing everything."

"So you let them hate her, too." Wade couldn't believe how far his brothers had been willing to go.

Her hand squeezed his and he looked down at her. Those big blue eyes of hers pleaded with him to let it go. She used to give him the same look when he would get into it with Brock. If he'd done as she'd asked back then, would the man have gotten as dangerously obsessed with her? At the time he'd been arrogant and thought he could handle anything, but she'd been the one to pay. He nodded and turned, not releasing her hand. "Let's go."

"Wade," his brother called out.

"Enjoy your honeymoon." He walked back to the hall, hefting his duffel with his free hand.

He led her out of the house where they'd become friends, kissed for the first time, cuddled together, made love. Where they should have been married, brought their babies home to visit.

With the sound of the party drifting across the lawn, he walked away from his home and didn't look back.

Chapter Three

Genny couldn't quite believe she was sitting in his truck. It felt surreal.

Somehow all these years later, she'd suspected he'd known. Even though Clint had told her he didn't, in the back of her mind she'd convinced herself that he'd known.

"Why?" He turned out of the long driveway onto the highway that led into town.

"Because I was a stupid kid and I thought love meant sacrifice," she replied, staring out the window. In the distance she could see the lights of the party. "You shouldn't be hard on Clint. He was a kid, too. A kid trying to take his father's place. He always tried to help me when he could."

"He should have told me the truth."

"I don't know. I think you would have lost your home and we still would have split up. We were too young to get married." She thought about it all the time. It had been foolish to think it could have worked. "Besides, I'd been willing to give up a lot for you. I don't know why this surprises you. I was a very naïve girl."

"You were still going to go to college," he said, his hands gripping the steering wheel with none of his usual grace. "I wasn't taking that away from you."

"I had a full ride to UT Austin," she pointed out. "I was walking away from that for you."

"We were going to build something special. We were going to have a family. I wouldn't have stopped you from getting your degree."

Something would have come along. She would have gotten pregnant or he would have been deployed or moved to another base.

Now that she looked back, she wished she could shake some sense into her younger self. "It doesn't matter. When you get into town, take a right. I'm in the trailer park outside of town."

"You're living in that rattrap trailer park?"

She sighed. "It's all I could afford. My dad died and he didn't leave us much except for the information I used to take down Brock. Dad had kept the books for the factory for years. He knew where all the secrets were buried. After Brock went to jail, the factory closed. There wasn't anything left. They sold it all off to pay Brock's debts. I'd signed a prenup so most of our personal assets are his. He made sure to hide the money we had left. Rattrap trailer park has to do until I can move and find a job. There's nothing for me here."

His hands tightened on the steering wheel. "I'm going to kill my brother."

Somehow she hadn't expected that reaction. "He tried to help. I wouldn't take more from him than I absolutely had to. I'm trying to get back into the workforce. Well, I'm trying to get into the workforce. I don't have a degree. I don't have experience. Working summers at a factory that shut down for corruption probably doesn't count."

"I'll get you a job."

She should have known that if he decided to say yes to her, he would take over. It was what he did. That cool competence had been one of the things that attracted her to him. At the time, she'd been young and unsure. Wade had seemed to know how to do everything, how to get the things he wanted. She'd followed. Now she couldn't follow. She had to take charge and save her son. "That's not what I need you to do. I need your professional services."

"You have them," he replied. "Can I ask the nature of the threat? Brock's in jail, correct?"

"Yes, but that hasn't stopped him." She shivered even though the cab was warm enough. "He blames me for going to jail."

"So he didn't embezzle a bunch of money?" Wade sounded like he knew the answer to that question.

"Oh, he did. He stole millions and gambled it all away. But he's right about me being the reason he went to jail. I gave the feds all the evidence I'd documented over the years. I was careful and I waited. I knew I had to get him on a federal level because he owned the county judges. He couldn't buy off the one in Houston."

"How many years had you been planning?"

"Since my son was born. I thought once the ranch was safely paid off, I would divorce him and get on with my life. He switched out my birth control pills. He says he didn't, but I'm almost sure that's how it happened. Once I had Asher, I couldn't leave without risking losing my son." She couldn't imagine what would have happened if her sweet boy had been raised by her monstrous mother-in-law. Brock hadn't cared about the child except as a control measure for her, but Emily Howard had wanted to twist Ash into her perfect grandchild.

It wasn't kind of her, but she'd been grateful when the old bat had a heart attack. Of course, then the leash had been off her husband, but at least Ash had been spared.

"I don't know what to say," Wade admitted. "I'm still reeling from finding out that all these years you'd been trying to save my family."

"It doesn't matter now." The past was the past.

"It does and I'll protect you with everything I have. We'll pack your things and you'll come with me to Dallas. My place is secure and I'll make it even more so. I'll have the boys come out and set up cameras and motion detectors. If it gets bad, I'll move you to the club while I handle the situation."

She didn't need him to do that. At least not for her. "I can handle the situation myself. I wasn't asking you to protect me. I need you to protect my son."

His jaw tightened. "Of course, I will. I'll protect both of you."

She watched him carefully, his face illuminated by the light from the dashboard. He'd tried to go stony, but for a mere second, she'd seen his distaste. His distaste for her son. Well, she should have expected that. In her mind, Wade was still some kind of all-American hero, despite the fact that he hadn't come back for her. She'd decided that had been for the best, but she hadn't expected his hatred for Brock to transfer to her son.

"I've changed my mind. I think we'll be fine." When Clint got back from his honeymoon, she would ask about Ash staying with him and Lori for a bit. Or maybe a long time, if things went wrong. If she went to jail, she'd already made arrangements. And if she died, well, she'd tried to make arrangements for that, too. "Drop me off at home and I'll get out of your hair."

She maintained her composure this time. Years of keeping a bland expression on her face even as she ached from some wound her husband had inflicted made it fairly easy. She wouldn't let him know how much it hurt inside that she couldn't trust him with her son.

"What did I do?" he asked quietly, his eyes on the road.

She thought about shrugging him off, but she'd moved past niceties and sparing others' feelings. "You can't stand the thought of my son."

He was silent for a moment, the truth sitting between them. "I'm thinking about him as Brock's son and that's hard for me. I know you won't believe me, but Clint was right. I never got over you. I tried. Believe me, I tried. I'm sure the night you sacrificed yourself to that bastard I was in some other woman's bed."

He was on the edge in a way she hadn't expected. She'd never heard that hitch in his voice, never heard him anything less than confident. "It's in the past."

"Maybe it is for you, but it just happened to me."

"You'll get over it."

He shook his head. "That's what I'm telling you. I never got over you. I never got over you when I thought you were some flighty bitch who picked money. What the hell do I do now that I realize you're practically a saint and I was fucking someone else, drinking and partying while you were being raped? Who the fuck am I?"

She'd thought she'd used up all her tears, but there they were. The truth was it felt good to cry, to feel anything at all. And to feel sympathy for him proved she hadn't lost her whole soul. But she was tired, so damn tired of all the pain, all the blame. "You're Wade Rycroft. You're the man you've become, and from what your brother says, that man is pretty incredible. You were a child. I was a child. We did foolish things. Drive me home and we can shake hands and maybe finally move on with our lives."

"I don't want to move on." He took a deep breath. "I'm sorry I had a bad reaction to thinking about your son. Your son. You're his momma and that means he's probably a spectacular kid and I'm going to watch over him. And you."

"It's late. I'm going to get some sleep and make a decision in the morning." The truth was if Ash was in Dallas being watched by a professional bodyguard, she would feel better about doing what she had to do. Still, she needed to consider the fact that Wade might be too close to the situation to be able to do the job.

"If you don't want me, I'll hire someone from my firm. Shane Landon is a good man and an excellent bodyguard. I would trust Shane with my life," he said.

"I can't afford to hire someone. I was coming to you because I thought you owed me."

He shook his head as he made the turn into her sad trailer park. "I'll take care of it. Let me stay with you tonight. I'll sleep on the couch. In the morning, we'll talk more."

That seemed like a bad idea, but she got the feeling he wasn't going to go back to his brother's and there weren't any motels in town. The nearest one was twenty miles away. It seemed wrong to make him drive that far when she was asking him for a costly favor. Besides, it would give her a chance to see if he could honestly be nice to her son.

She shouldn't make emotional decisions. Hadn't she learned that a long time ago? "All right. Though I'll warn you, the couch is pretty crappy. It's really more of a love seat."

"I can handle it." He let out a breath as though he was happy to not have to fight her on that one.

"I'm the single wide at the end of the lane on the right."

He pulled in front, the headlights illuminating the sad state of her living arrangements. He stared at the dilapidated trailer for a moment.

"You're thinking about killing your brother again, aren't you?" It was odd. Sitting beside him made her feel more like herself than she had in years. How long had it been since she'd joked with anyone but Ash? And that was all about making sure he wasn't scared, keeping his spirits up.

"I can feel his throat in my hands," he agreed.

"If it makes you feel any better, he and Lori offered me a room at the house. They also offered to put me up in an apartment."

"Why didn't you let them?"

For so many reasons. "I need to stand on my own at some point. I need to build something of my own, something for me and Ash."

"This isn't properly built, Gen."

Laughter bubbled up inside her. It was ridiculous. It was surreal. Maybe this plan of hers could work. Maybe she could find a way. Or maybe she would be in jail or dead, but in that moment, she wanted to laugh at the ridiculousness of it all. "It's horrible and I like it way better than that damn mansion. The heater doesn't work at all and it's still warmer."

Wade killed the engine and turned in his seat. "Genny?"

With a long sigh, she sat back. "Not tonight. We'll talk in the morning. I can't do anything else tonight. I'll answer all your questions in the morning."

"All right." He opened the door and got out.

Before she could get her own door open, he was there helping her to the ground. She couldn't resist putting her hand in his and letting him help her down. His big hand encompassed hers, warmth flooding her system. She forced herself to let go when her feet were firmly planted on the ground. "Thanks. I'll introduce you to Ash. Just to prepare you, he wasn't in a good mood when I left. He thinks he's far too old to have a babysitter, but I wouldn't leave him alone."

He nodded, staring at the trailer in front of him. At least it was clean on the inside. She'd gotten a lot of Lori's old furniture when her friend had moved into the Rycroft ranch. Once she got Wade inside, he might stop thinking about how poor she was.

He stopped at the base of the stairs that led to the door. "Genny, thank you for giving me another chance."

She wasn't sure how to answer that because the last thing they had was a second chance. Still, she opened the door and invited him inside.

* * * *

Wade watched as the door closed behind the older woman who'd been watching over Asher. He was almost sure the woman had a gun and holster under her sweater. Genny was afraid. He needed to figure out what Brock was doing to scare her from a prison cell.

Genny locked the door, making sure she latched the chain that wouldn't actually keep anyone who wanted in out. The door itself was flimsy. If the windows locked, he would be surprised. He needed to get her out of here if there was any kind of threat at all.

"Mom?"

She turned and for the first time all night, he saw her face light up in a genuine way. "Hey, baby. How was your night?"

Asher Howard was roughly thirteen years old, with the skinny body of a boy who wasn't even close to becoming a man. He was almost the same height as his mother, and that wasn't where the similarities ended.

The kid had dark hair that needed a cut and clear blue eyes that mirrored his mother's. Wade couldn't help but stare because if there was a drop of his father in him, he couldn't see it. That child was Genny's.

Genny had a son. He'd dreamed of having kids with her and here was her son. She was asking him to protect her child.

"Mavis is surprisingly good at Xbox." He looked across the tiny living room and his eyes widened. "Wade Rycroft?"

"Yes." Damn, but he looked like his mom. "That's me. I'm an old high school friend of your mother's."

"You were her high school boyfriend. You were the reason why she married my father, though I firmly believe dear old Dad would have found another way. If it hadn't been you he used as leverage, it would have been my grandfather. But you could have come back for her. That was a dick move."

Genny's jaw dropped. "Ash!"

"No, he's right. It *was* a dick move." He crossed the space between them and held out a hand. "One I won't make again. It's good to meet you, Ash."

The boy solemnly shook his hand. "It's good to meet you. Thanks for coming with her. I was worried she would pull a gun on you."

This was good. Genny went a bright pink and Wade was starting to understand that the kid knew his mom well. "She did. And then she attacked me and then I found out what a dick I'd been. It was a rough night, but tomorrow we're going to talk about getting the two of you out of here."

Ash shot his mom a quizzical stare. "You didn't tell him?"

"Tell me what?" Wade asked.

"We'll talk about everything in the morning. For tonight, let's settle in. I'll get the extra sheets and make the couch up." She disappeared down the hall.

Ash turned somber eyes his way. "Are you going to say yes? Are you going to take care of us?"

That stare. He knew it well. Genny had to love this kid so fucking much. If they'd gotten married, the kid in front of him would be his, and suddenly it was easy to look past who his father was. He had another chance with Genny. It had been all he'd been able to think about on the way here. He'd screwed up. He hadn't been faithful and true to her. "Yes. I don't understand the situation, but I'm going to do everything I can to protect you and your mom. I take it this is about your dad."

"Biological donor," Ash corrected. "I watched him beat her. He is not my dad."

He took a deep breath, trying to push his anger at Brock down. His anger at a lot of people was bubbling up, but this wasn't the place. "I won't let him touch her again."

Ash nodded. "All right then. I'm going to make some tea. Mom likes herbal tea before bedtime. I know this place looks shitty, but it's the best. No one watching us all the time. Mac and cheese is great, you know. Mavis made some for dinner. It's quite delicious. She made cookies, too. Chocolate chip. I'm totally addicted to sugar. I didn't understand it before."

Wade thought about leaning against the bar but worried it wouldn't hold his weight. "You sound like you've never had them."

Ash filled a kettle with water from the sink before settling it on the ancient stove and turning on the burner. "Never. Not until Brock went to jail. The Howards are serious about proper nutrition. I wasn't allowed anything that wasn't on Grandmother's list of acceptable foods. She would say my mother's genes could run true, and she wouldn't have a fattie for a grandson. Brock kept it up after she died. The day he went to jail my mom took me to get a burger and fries and a milkshake. I was sick all night and it was worth it. I'm on what I like to call an extended food tour. I've been working my way through the candy aisle whenever we have some extra cash. And cake. Mom bought me a birthday cake even though my birthday isn't for a few months. But I want to try more flavors. I liked the yellow cake."

The kid had never had candy or cake? No chocolate bunny on Easter or cupcakes at a party? "I have a friend who makes some of the best desserts you've ever tasted. He works in a restaurant. He used to be in the Army, but now he's a pastry chef."

Ash's eyes lit up. "Cool. He can kill people and bake cookies."

The kettle started to whistle and Ash pulled down a couple of mugs. "Would you like some tea?"

He shook his head. "Nah. I'm not much of a tea guy."

"Here we go." Genny walked in from the hallway, a set of sheets in her hand. She glanced over as Ash was prepping her tea. "Thanks, sweetie. I appreciate it."

"Ash was telling me about his food tour." He said the words lightly but he was serious. He wanted to know how bad it had gotten. Had she been put through the same things?

Her shoulders got tight, her eyes focusing on the couch and her task. "He's enjoying some of the freedom we've found. Brock was very controlling. I'm sure he would tell you it was because he wanted the best for his family."

"It was because he was a massive asshole," Ash replied with a smile. "Here, you drink your tea and I'll make up the couch."

"You have to stop cussing," she said with a sigh, taking the tea. "Freedom doesn't mean you get to do anything you want."

The kid shrugged. "I only use those words when nothing else will do. Sit down, Mom."

Genny eased onto one of the barstools and took a sip of tea. She glanced up at him, apology in her eyes. "Sorry. He's still adjusting to life outside the mansion, as we call it."

He focused on her, taking in the subtle ways she'd changed. "It sounds like life inside the mansion wasn't very good."

She nodded, taking another drink of tea. "It was insufferable, but it's over and we get to move on. I know I said you owe me tonight, but I don't want you to feel guilty about this. My son is probably right. Brock would have found something else to use against me. He meant to have me one way or another."

"I always knew he was interested in you in a way you didn't understand. I didn't think he was obsessed with you." No matter what she said, guilt formed a hard kernel in his gut, weighing him down. It was hard to believe that when he'd woken up this morning he'd thought he'd known how the world worked. Now it was all confused. "I thought it was about me. He hated me since we were kids."

"He hated all of you," she replied, holding the mug in both hands. "Your brothers and your family. It took me a long time to figure it out. At first I thought it was because you were more popular. Brock was the son of the wealthiest family in town and that made people tread cautiously around him, but it didn't help him find friends. He was always weird. I grew up with him. I was used to his odd mannerisms, but the kids in school made fun of him."

"Yeah, well, kids don't like the kid who costs them cupcakes," Ash added. "Kindergartners are mean and believe in a certain amount of biblical justice. I still have a scar from that rock."

Genny hid a yawn behind her hand. "His grandmother ruled the school. Any class Ash was in had a set of rules meant to keep him on his diet and turn him into a proper Howard. She would have sent him to boarding school but she was worried that she'd made a mistake doing it with Brock. Like I said, Brock was fairly under control until his mother died, but she knew he was violent."

Wade didn't want to think about how bad it had been for Ash. It was easier to focus on Brock. "I can't say I was friendly with him. I was a kid. He was mean. The first time I remember ever seeing him, he was torturing a dog. I was eight or nine and put him on his ass and took the dog with me. The sheriff came out to the ranch and explained to my parents that if I ever touched the kid again, they'd send me to juvie."

"Well, that's why he hated you. You made him feel small," she said softly.

"Everything and everyone made him feel small." Ash moved to his mother's side. "It's because he was small. He had a small mind and I'm sure he has a tiny little…"

Genny slapped her hand over her only child's mouth. "Don't you even." Her eyes were sleepy and she yawned again. "Wow. I got tired really fast."

Wade noticed Ash hadn't done what he'd said he would do. The sheets were still neatly folded on the couch. Well, he could do it himself. "Why don't you go on to bed? I can handle things out here."

He wouldn't sleep a wink. He would sit up all night long thinking about what she'd been through, wondering if things could have been different if he'd tried harder, believed in her more.

"Or you could go ahead and pass out," Ash urged. "It'll make things easier."

What had he done? Wade looked from the mug in Genny's hand back to the counter. Sure enough, there was a small bottle of medication sitting there.

Genny sighed and her eyes were unfocused. "Something's wrong. I didn't drink much at the wedding. I only had the one drink. Why is my brain fuzzy?"

"Because I slipped you a mickey, as they would say in some noir film. It's okay. I checked the dosage. You'll be out for eight to ten hours," Ash assured her. "You can use the sleep."

"What the hell?" Wade rushed over to the bottle. They were

sleeping pills prescribed to Genny, but the date was months old and it looked like she'd never used them. Until her son decided she needed some bedtime.

"Wade? I don't think I can get to bed." The words slurred as she pushed back from her chair.

He managed to catch her before she hit the floor. She weighed next to nothing in his arms. There was a reason her clothes didn't fit her. She was too thin, and not in a naturally healthy way. He clutched her to his chest and looked for the kid he was about to have a serious talk with. Maybe there was more of his father in there than he'd thought.

"In the morning, she was going to tell you to take me to Dallas," Ash explained quietly. "She never intended to go with us. Brock gets out of prison any day now and he's going to come after both of us. She's going to lie in wait and she's going to kill him. I can't allow that to happen because she'll either lose that battle or go to jail. We need you. You're a bodyguard. You work for one of the premier security firms in the world. I can't pay you but I'm begging you to save my mom."

"She's going to try to kill him?" The words didn't make sense. Genny was gentle. Genny had worried about him going into the military because deep down she'd been a pacifist. The idea of her lying in wait to murder her ex didn't compute.

"Yes," Ash said. "I'm sorry for taking this choice away from her. She's had very few of them, but I can't allow her to ruin the rest of her life because she's protecting me. It might not be fair, but I'm putting it on you. You loved her once. You could love her again."

"I never stopped loving her," he admitted. "But there's a difference between saying she's going to kill someone and actually doing it."

"She's got a will in place that gives custody of me to Clint and Lori."

He felt like he'd been kicked in the gut. She was planning on doing it. She was going to try to go out in a blaze of glory. His eyes met Asher's, a moment of pure connection and harmony between the men.

"Pack a bag for your mother. I suspect you're already ready," Wade said. "We're going to Dallas."

Ash was moving before he finished the sentence.

He looked down at the woman in his arms and promised she would be alive at the end of this.

Chapter Four

Genny came awake slowly, her brain a bit on the foggy side. And then she kind of sighed and stretched. She was still dreaming because she was in some kind of heavenly bed. The one she slept in now was hard as a rock and still had metal springs. But this, this was paradise. Her back didn't hurt and she was warm. And she could smell Wade.

Definitely dreaming. If she was dreaming she would make the most of it. She reached out, hoping to feel his muscular chest under her hand. All she met with was more quilt.

Even in her dreams she was far away from him.

"Real maple syrup is the only way to go," a masculine voice said from a distance. "And I have to admit I don't mind putting some chocolate chips in. Now there are people in my life who tell me that means I eat like a five-year-old, but I'm okay with that."

"Seriously? Chocolate chip pancakes? I love the world." She knew that voice. Her baby boy.

A husky laugh followed. "I'll make you love it more. We're sitting down and watching some movies this afternoon. I've got to educate you, kid. You're sure you've never seen *Jurassic Park*?"

"Entertainment was not high on the list of Howard priorities. I watched a lot of documentaries, but mostly TV and movies weren't allowed in the house."

Her heart ached at the sound of her son's voice.

And then it hardened because she remembered what had happened the night before. She sat up in bed, taking in her surroundings as the truth flooded her brain. She'd been in her trailer, drinking tea and talking to Wade. It had been weird to see Wade in her tiny trailer, but she'd felt safer than she had in years with him there. It had been an illusion because she was never safe and wouldn't be until Brock was taken out, but she'd sat on her rickety barstool and decided to pretend for a night. Then she'd gotten woozy.

Ash had put something in her drink. He'd even told her he'd done it.

Where the hell were they? She glanced around the room. It was fairly utilitarian, with a bed covered by a quilt, a dresser with a mirror, and one chair. The place was neat but there wasn't a lot of personality to it. Definitely decorated by a man, and not one who cared about making things pretty. There were no brightly colored throws or art on the walls. The lamp on the bedside table was simple. On the dresser were two framed photos. One was of the Rycroft brothers. The second was Wade and a group of men. There were seven of them, all with beers in one hand and flipping the bird at whomever was taking the picture.

She was at Wade's place. She glanced back toward the bed where a nightstand sat on the right side. There was a digital clock reading 10:20. AM, obviously. She'd slept almost twelve hours? She hadn't slept more than four or five hours a night in years. Well, at least she knew the damn drugs worked. Someone had gotten her out of her dress and put her in a completely oversized T-shirt. Now she knew why she smelled like Wade.

But he hadn't shared the bed with her. The left side of the bed was smooth and unused. He'd given it to her and she would bet anything he'd been the one to change her clothes. Ash would do a lot for her, but he would have left her in the dress she'd worn. Wade had left her in her bra and undies, but they were comfortable enough.

It couldn't stand. They'd shoved her in Wade's truck and taken her to Dallas against her will, though she allowed Wade might not have understood her will. She hadn't wanted to get into a fight with him the night before and had left the discussion of how things would work until the morning. Still, she had to put her foot down. Wade felt guilty now, but she couldn't count on anyone. Too much was at stake, and at some point Wade would figure out Brock had simply been determined and it was a mere twist of fate that made him the vehicle to force her to his side.

And she was ready to have a serious talk with her son.

Except she couldn't find her clothes. Screw it. She was angry enough that the part of her legs they saw wouldn't matter. The T-shirt was like a mini dress. She strode through the door and into the hallway.

The heavenly smell of bacon hit her nose.

God, it had been forever since she'd had bacon. Brock had put her on a diet the day they married. He'd controlled what she ate, who she saw, what she did. And then after Brock had gone to jail, she had to pay for everything with what little she had. They'd been eating ramen noodles and boxed pasta for months.

Tears pierced her eyes, clouding her vision. She wanted this life for her son, a life where bacon and pancakes were normal, where no one ground him into the dirt if he rebelled, where the authority figure in his life wanted to watch movies with him.

But it was dangerous for her to stay here. Ash might be able to have those things, but until she did what she needed to do, she couldn't begin to dream about it for herself.

She took a deep breath and strode in, pointing her finger at her criminally-minded child. "You are grounded."

Ash held his hands up. "I'm really glad Wade still has your gun."

Wade was standing at the stove. He'd forgotten to put on his shirt and it was all she could do to not drool. That man was fine. The promise of his youth had been fulfilled. He was all muscle, his chest covered with tan skin and some scars that spoke of years with the Green Berets. His jeans were worn and hung low on his hips. And he had the most phenomenal ass she'd ever seen on a man. "Hey, good morning, princess. I'm sorry about the mickey. I would like to note for the record that I had no knowledge of what was coming and I managed to catch you before you hit the floor. Coffee?"

He was acting like this was some joke they would laugh about. "You knew where you were going. You knew I wasn't conscious when you shoved me in your truck and drove me away from my home."

He flipped a pancake neatly in the pan. "That rickety trailer wasn't a home. It was a set of accidents waiting to happen. And I'm pretty sure someone was cooking meth in that place. I did not shove you anywhere. I was very gentle. I gently laid you in the back of the cab and belted you in for safety. Ash manipulated the situation so I was the only adult left who could make decisions. After careful consideration, I decided I could either call the police on the kid or bring you both up here and start his rehabilitation. Besides, you told me we would talk in the morning. It's morning."

"He's totally right about that," Ash said.

"You keep quiet and maybe you'll see the light of day in a couple of years." She turned to Wade. "I need to go back."

A single brow rose on Wade's handsome face. "To that dilapidated trailer? There's no security there. It's safer for you here by far. I've already got a couple of calls in to friends around town. We've got a meeting with the principal of the local middle school first thing Monday. I'm taking a week off to get you two settled in."

The temptation to let him take over was so great. "Ash can stay. That was my plan all along."

"Which was why I had to slip you that sleeping pill," Ash added. He winced when she looked his way. "Did I mention I was scared, Mommy?"

She couldn't talk to him right now. "Don't you even play that with me. You knew I had a plan. You know I've spent months studying up on him to make sure he's the right man to watch over you. You don't get to ruin the plan because you don't agree with me." Months and months she'd spent first talking to Clint and Lori and then spending what little money she had to get a report on her former lover. She had to make sure he hadn't changed in the long years they'd been apart. She turned to the man she knew would take care of her son. "Wade, I will sign everything I need to in order to get him into a good school, but I need to be in Broken Bend."

"Why?" Wade asked the question like he already knew the answer.

"I have to be there when Brock gets out of jail. We have things to work out." It wasn't exactly a lie. They needed to work out his death. When he had a bullet in him, maybe she could come back for her son. And if not, she'd made plans for him. The one thing that wasn't going to happen was Ash going back to his father.

"I have that handled," Wade said smoothly. "We're going to talk to a lawyer on Tuesday. His name is Mitchell and he's a friend of mine. He's very terse and not all that friendly, but you'll like his wife and he's excellent at what he does."

"I'm already divorced." She didn't see what a lawyer could do.

"Mitch can try to revamp the custody agreement," Wade explained. "Right now it's fifty fifty, correct?"

So Ash had been talking. "Yes. Despite the fact that he was under indictment at the time. I was terrified he would take Ash and run. I was relieved when they revoked his bail. He flew to Mexico to meet with some business associates when he was under strict orders not to leave the county."

"I turned him in," Ash said with a smile. "And then told him it was safe to come home. I'm an excellent actor. For years I've played the dutiful son and it finally paid off. It was beautiful when they met his plane and hauled him away in handcuffs."

"Yeah, well, the local judge still granted him joint custody. I think he might have given him full if there hadn't been a bunch of press at the time." The fact that a great deal of Texas knew the story had been the only thing that had saved her. Brock and his family had controlled the local legal system for a long time. "Clint made that happen. He pressed the local papers to cover the story and it got picked up in Houston and San Antonio."

"Clint made a lot of things happen," Wade replied, his eyes narrowing.

"I love it when he does that," Ash said with a grin. "It's super intimidating. His eyes are like lasers. I've gotta learn how to do that. Mom, you were right. He's awesome. He can kill a man like twenty different ways and he makes great pancakes."

Heat flashed through her system. "I didn't say he was awesome. I merely said he was capable of taking care of you."

Wade's gorgeous face split into a breathtaking smile. "I'm glad you think so because that's exactly what I plan to do. Take care of you. Both of you. There's no need for you to ever be in a room with that bastard again. Definitely not alone. And Mitch is going to attempt to get the case moved here to Dallas. He can make the argument that you've begun a new life here in a place where the scandal can't touch your son and where you can make a decent living. You start your job at McKay-Taggart next Monday. Nice salary and benefits."

Her head was spinning, and not because she'd been drugged. "A job? I have a job? I can't have a job. I don't even think I have clothes."

"Wade's figured that out, too. You're going shopping with some of his friends' wives," Ash explained. "I am, too. I need a flashy wardrobe if I'm going to make a splash in the new school. I've decided to go with mysterious newcomer. Is he a Hollywood star undercover? Or perhaps an operative out to save the school. Wade says women like a little mystery. I'm totally into bacon. I think it's time for me to move on to other things I was forbidden. I want to pick up some chicks."

Oh, dear lord. She wanted to watch him blossom into the wild, imaginative, loving man she knew he could be. She'd done one good thing in the last fifteen years and now he was going to spread his wings. And she wouldn't watch it because she had to ensure that he could live and thrive. Wade could bring in anyone he liked, but she knew Brock always won in the end. If she gave him the confrontation he would want, maybe he would leave their son alone. "I would like to know where my dress and purse are. I'll get myself home."

"Genny," Wade began.

Ash had lost the grin and gone pale. She'd seen that look on his face far too many times. It aged him and reminded her that he was old beyond his years. He had been forced to act, to pretend in order to protect them both. She'd taught him how to make himself nearly invisible, how to pick his battles. "Mom, I'd like to talk to you before you go. I packed some clothes for you and I'll give you the bag if you'll talk to me for a moment."

Yeah, she'd probably taught him that, too. Too much of her life had been a negotiation, finding any kind of leverage she could in order to get the tiniest of compromises from her husband. "All right, but you've always known I never meant to leave Broken Bend until I deal with Brock."

"And I've always known I was going to stop you," he replied.

Wade had turned around, focusing on the bacon, his back to them as though he was giving them space.

She walked through the small kitchen into Wade's living room. The house wasn't large, but it had great bones. Though she hadn't seen the outside, she would bet it was an older home, perhaps built in the seventies or early eighties. A ranch house because that's what he would be comfortable in. The living room was sadly devoid of anything decorative.

Shouldn't a girlfriend have fixed this place up? It had real potential, but there was no warmth in the leather lounge chairs and massive TV. There were two chairs and a sad little TV tray between them. Though he seemed to have invested heavily in remotes and video game systems.

She turned to her son. Wade's lack of style wasn't her problem. Ash was. "I can't believe you drugged me and thought you could get away with it. Do you have any idea what could have happened if you hadn't gotten the dosage right? How could you do that to me?"

"First of all, I can read, and I wasn't worried that it would hurt you. That medication was prescribed by a doctor for you. You're the one who's too stubborn to use it." Ash crossed his arms over his chest. "And secondly, how could you do *this* to me?"

Yep, it was like arguing with herself. "I'm doing this *for* you and you know it. I have to deal with your father. He won't simply get out of jail and go on about his life. He's going to come after us. If you're safe, then I believe he'll only come after me. I've been his obsession for years."

"I know that. Let Wade deal with him. He wants to. I think Wade would love to spend some time dealing with Brock."

She was sure he would, but she wasn't putting this on Wade. He'd made his choice long ago. "It's not his problem."

Asher paced, a sure sign he was anxious. "He's willing to make it his problem. None of this means anything if you're dead at the end. Or if you're in jail. We've spent years planning how we would get away. You've spent years promising me what our lives would be like if we could get away. I want that life and I can't have it without you."

His voice cracked at the end, a reminder of how young her baby was, how much of his youth had been stolen away.

Her heart ached, but she couldn't back down. She had to do everything she could to protect him. She wanted him to have that life. He could have it without her. "You won't have anything at all if you don't let me do what I need to do."

"But that's the point," he shot back. "You don't have to do anything. You want to. You want to be the one who takes him out. You want to be the reason he goes down, and you can be, but you don't have to do it yourself. You don't have to be the one who pulls the trigger."

"I can't trust anyone else."

He stopped and stared at her. "Bullshit."

"Stop, Ash. You have to stop the cursing."

He shrugged. "Why? Why should I listen to a word you say? You want to leave. Fine. Go, but you don't get to have any say over what I do with my life if you're not willing to be my mom."

He was attempting to put her in a corner, but he didn't understand. "I'm trying to be your mother."

He shook his head. "Again, I call bullshit. You're leaving me behind. You think you can pawn me off on someone and then finish this war Brock started. You won't win. Even if you manage to kill him, you'll go to jail for the rest of your life. They don't allow you to kill a man because he used to abuse you. Either you're going to set something sketchy up or you're going to let him get close enough that it's a real fight. You'll lose a real fight. The chance of you coming out of this alive and free is not worth the risk."

"Baby, letting him potentially get custody of you isn't worth the risk."

He wasn't having any of it. "If you're dead, he'll get custody and you won't be here to fight for me. I'll be alone, and I don't know that I can handle that."

The corner he was pushing her into was getting smaller and smaller, and she didn't like the way he was making her feel. She was doing this for him, damn it. "You won't be alone. I've made arrangements in case something goes wrong."

"I don't want an arrangement. Mom, please don't do this. You promised me. I want to mean more to you than revenge against him. We did it. We got away. Can't that be enough?"

"It's not about revenge." But some of the things he was saying made sense. Wade was the security expert. If she trusted him to protect her son, why would he be incapable of watching out for her, too?

"Cool, then we can stay here and be normal for as long as we can." Ash had turned on what she liked to think of as his life coach mode. He got animated and encouraging when he was trying to get her to do something big. "I like Wade. He's surprisingly cool for an old military dude. I like this place. I want to go to school and have friends and watch movies, but more than anything else, I want to see my mom happy. This path you've put us on, it won't make either one of us happy. What's freedom worth if there's no joy in it? If we're not together. I wasn't playing you. I am scared, Mom. Please. You've spent my whole life sacrificing for me. Live for me. Live with me. Let's stay right here and let Wade watch out for us. He can teach us. He's already promised to teach me some self-defense and let me go to the gym with him. You can come with us."

Go with him and Wade? Like they were some kind of family? She couldn't. She shook her head. "I can't trust him."

"This is about Wade? Because if you think you don't have anything to offer him, take a look around this place. You could turn this into a home for him."

"That's not the issue. I'm not playing housewife for him." Even though the truth was she'd already started thinking about it. Deep down she'd always wondered what her home with Wade would have been like. Not as grand as the Howard Mansion, but warm and comfortable and filled with happiness.

Ash seemed to think, like he hadn't considered that side of the problem. "All right. I'll get our things. I honestly thought he was what's best for us, for you, but I won't force you into even a friendship with a man you don't like. You should understand something though. I'm going with you and if you leave me behind, I'll find a way to get back to you. I'll be beside you when Brock shows up. Do you remember what you said to me when I was seven and I realized he was hitting you?"

"I said none of it mattered as long as you were with me. I told you that no pain was too much as long as I had you. I said we were a team and no one could break us." The tears fell and there was nothing she could do to stop them.

Ash stepped up, his hands on her shoulders. "Nothing matters as long as you're with me. I can take the pain if I have you. We're a team and nothing and no one gets to break us. Not even you."

"I don't dislike Wade," she said quietly. It was clear to her now. She was using Brock as an excuse. "I'm scared of him. I loved him once, but he didn't love me the same way. I'm scared if I stay here, he'll hurt me again. I guess I was in that life for so long I don't know anything else, baby. What if I'm not any good at being your mom out here in the real world? I can't even get you to stop cussing."

Suddenly he was in her arms, and despite the fact that he was now slightly taller than she was, she could feel the child he'd been. She could see him when he'd first been born, small and needy and world changing. She could see him at two, clinging to her; at five, already somber because he knew the rules. The rules were gone and the world had opened up for them both.

What did she want? Did she want to avenge the past at the cost of a possible future? She'd spent her whole adult life choosing her son over everything else. She could say this was about him, but deep inside her heart she knew this was all about Brock and her. This was about finishing something. But it would finish her, too. It would finish the team she'd formed with her son.

They had a chance here, but only if she was willing to give Wade some trust. They'd been friends before they'd been lovers. Perhaps they could find that again.

She kissed her son on the cheek. "All right. We can stay."

Ash let go, his eyes widening as she walked back into the kitchen. Wade was still there, plating pancakes.

She sat down at his bistro table. It was really made for two. They would need a bigger one. Maybe she could get a couple of houseplants to bring some color into this bland kitchen. "I appreciate all the work you've done this morning. I do need some clothes. I'll pay you back when I can. Could I have some coffee, please?"

He tripped over his own feet to get it for her.

Ash walked back, carrying a folding chair. "He doesn't have a lot of furniture."

"I didn't need it," Wade admitted, putting the mug in front of her. "But we've got a week to make the place comfy. And I have access to Clint's bank account. Everything's on him, and you're not paying his ass back."

She had to work on that, too. She wasn't going to be the reason Wade didn't speak to his brother. She took a long drink of the coffee. It was rich and warm and comforting.

A little like the man at the stove.

Ash started talking about everything he needed for school and Wade placed plates in front of them both and then joined them. He smiled and laughed, encouraging her to take the last of the bacon.

It was pretty much everything she'd dreamed a family could be.

And Genny realized she might be in trouble.

* * * *

Wade stepped out onto the back porch, shutting the door behind him. It had been a deeply satisfying day. After breakfast, they'd cleaned the kitchen and gone shopping, first to buy Asher new clothes and shoes and school supplies, and then to the grocery store. He'd pushed the cart as Genny and Asher had argued over what she would cook for the rest of the week. He'd wanted nothing but mac and cheese and pizza. She'd argued for healthy fare. Momma won. They would be eating a lot of chicken and fish, and he was looking forward to all of it. Especially the chocolate cake she'd promised as a compromise with her son.

The night was peaceful. Moonlight shone down, revealing the woman currently sitting on his porch swing. Genny stared out over his yard with its outdoor kitchen and hot tub. It was precisely why he'd bought this place. He loved sitting out here, having his friends over for barbecues and tossing a football around. Somewhere in the back of his mind, he'd thought this was a home where he could start a family. Of course, he'd never found the right woman.

Probably because the right woman had always been her.

"Hey, Ash is all bedded down. He's excited about school. I have to admit I find that interesting. At his age I would have used any excuse to get out of it." He walked over to the outdoor fridge. It was super cold, far colder than the one in his kitchen. It was where he kept his beer. He pulled two out. "You want one?"

"Absolutely. Three hours of being forced to give my opinion on how my son's ass looks in jeans and whether or not I would want to do that if I were a teenaged girl has taken a toll. I don't think that was normal, Wade."

He was fairly certain there wasn't a whole lot of normal about Ash, but damn, he liked the kid. He hadn't been able to help overhearing Ash's talk this morning with his mom. His heart had ached the whole time they'd worked out their differences, and had ached more when he'd realized he was one of those differences. "He's a great kid, Genny. He's a remarkable kid."

Her lips turned up as she took the beer from his hand. "Nothing at all like his dad."

"I think Ash would tell you that's all biology and meaningless to who he is on the inside." He sat down next to her, the swing creaking under his weight but holding steady.

"Ash says a lot of things." She tipped back her beer and was silent for a moment. "Am I doing the right thing?"

At least she was talking to him. She'd been perfectly polite when they'd gone to the mall shopping, but he could sense the careful distance she'd placed between them. He needed to reassure her. God, he needed to find a way to convince her to trust him again. "The school has excellent security. They've got CCTV on every hall and in the cafeteria. The campus itself has two police officers assigned to it. We're going to talk to the principal about our worries and the police will be made very aware of the threats."

"I don't think we can legally keep Brock away from the school. He's got partial custody," she replied.

"He won't after Mitch is through with him." He'd talked to Mitch earlier in the day. Though he mostly worked on contracts and corporate law, he could handle himself in any courtroom. Mitch loved to take down an asshole. He considered it a hobby of his. "And you have to remember, this is Dallas, not Broken Bend. I know your first instinct is to try to fix things yourself because you don't trust the system there. Brock isn't the one with power and influence here. My boss and his friends are very influential. The cops here won't care who Brock is. They'll take him down if he steps out of line."

She held the longneck against her chest as though trying to cool off. "I hope that's true because he will come after me and Asher. He'll try to take Ash to hurt me, to make me do what he wants. And I wasn't really talking about the school. He has to go to school. He's like me at that age. School was awesome. No, I'm worried staying here is a mistake."

"Because you can't trust me?" He tried to keep the bitterness out of his tone. He wasn't bitter with her. He was angry with himself, with all the years they'd lost. The crazy thing was his first instinct had been to storm home and force her to explain herself. But he'd been in the middle of boot camp, unable to leave. By the time he was able to go home, he'd talked himself into not speaking with her. Of course, she'd been married by then. Brock had known exactly what he was doing.

She sighed, a weary sound. "We're different people now."

"Maybe I am but you're not. Oh, you might be older but you're still the woman who would be so loyal to the boy she loved that she would give up her life. The only thing that's changed is the boy you love," he said. He'd thought about it all day, thought about how truly little she'd changed. She'd gone through hell and wasn't bitter, was still capable of love and forgiveness. Fuck, he didn't deserve her, but he was taking this chance. "I didn't deserve your loyalty. Neither did my brother or my mother." She started to open her mouth. He had to shut that down. "Don't. Don't tell me how to feel. I know you've worked through this, but I don't know how to."

"It helps to admit that we were all children back then."

"My mother wasn't." He needed to talk about this with her.

"No, but she wasn't the same after your dad died. She was lost and

I've forgiven her," she replied quietly. "You can't spend your life being angry."

"You're angry with me."

For a moment he thought she would ignore him. Then she turned to him, her eyes shining in the moonlight. "Maybe. It's hard to figure out how I feel about you. For a long time, I dreamed about you at night. You were the only man I ever loved. Brock killed that. I think he might have killed the part of me that can love someone other than my son. I didn't feel a lot when my father passed. But then he was the one who told me to suck it up. I went to him after Brock hit me the first time. He told me to not make my husband mad."

"Genny, he should have killed him. I would have. God, I should have." That sorrow that had been building inside him threatened to spill over. Anger was there, but it was overshadowed by the terrible pain he felt at the thought of her being alone and afraid.

"It's funny," she said, studying him in the silvery light. "I went over pretty much every possible scenario I could, and this wasn't the way I thought you would handle it. It's why it took forever for me to talk to you. I thought you would either not care at all or that you would be so angry you went after everyone. I hesitated because I thought I might unleash a beast."

He could give her this. Since the moment he'd learned the truth, he'd genuinely forced himself to think about how he reacted. It would be selfish to act out in anger when she needed him to be calm, to think about what was best for her. The drive from Broken Bend to Dallas with Ash had made that clear to him. They needed someone who would thoughtfully protect them, not a raging animal who fed his own needs. "You've had enough anger in your life. It's there. God, it's there, but I swear I won't act on it because I won't do anything that could hurt you. I'll try to handle him in every legal way I can and if I have to take him out, I'll do it in a way that can never come back on any of us. You don't need my rage. You do need me though."

"I don't want to."

"Because you think I'll let you down again." It wasn't a question.

"Because I don't want to love anyone again," she admitted. "I don't want to depend on anyone. I thank you for everything you're doing, but we can't stay here forever. When we know we're safe, Ash and I have to find our own place."

He didn't like the sound of that. "I won't force you to stay, but I'll do everything I can in the meantime to change your mind. I'll sleep on the air mattress for as long as you need me to, but you should know where I want to be. I won't play games with you and I won't manipulate you. You deserve honesty. I want you, Genny. I want you in my life, in my arms, in my bed. My plan is to make it so nice for you that you never want to leave. I want to make you feel safe and comfortable, and one day you'll wake up and this will be your home and it won't make sense to leave."

Her eyes shone in the moonlight. "It's not going to happen. I can be friends with you, but I don't think I can do the rest. He killed that part of me, too."

"Then I'll bring it back to life. I know it's ridiculous to compare our experiences. I won't even try, but I've lived a half-life since the day I lost you. I don't want to live that way anymore. My home, my heart, everything I have is yours. You only have to ask for it. You need someone to hold you, I'm here. You want kisses, these lips are yours. And I'll be more patient than you can imagine because this is the most important fight of my life. You and Ash already mean the world to me and I've known that kid for a whole twenty-four hours. I love him. I want to be in his life and yours."

Had he gone too far? Was she about to get up and walk away? He shouldn't have pushed her but he couldn't not tell her. He couldn't pretend. She deserved to know exactly what he was going to do and to talk about it all. He couldn't take another choice from her.

If she bolted, he would still watch over her.

"And if I never ask?"

She wasn't moving, wasn't walking away. He would take that as a victory for now. "It doesn't matter. I'll still want you here. I'll still want to be in your life."

She nodded and looked out over the yard. "Your backyard is way nicer than the inside of your house. Typical man. And I should sleep on the air mattress."

"Absolutely not, and you feel free to do anything you like to the house. I've never had a girlfriend live with me. I had a roommate for a while, but he got his own place and got married. I don't know about things like decorating. The only reason I can cook was pure necessity."

"You've never lived with a woman?"

"No." He'd never wanted to. Every time he came close, something made him hold back. Now he was pretty sure that something had been her.

She went back to silence, the only sound between them the slight squeaking the swing made and the hum of the hot tub. After a long moment, she spoke. "Do you remember when we used to do this on your porch?"

God, this was why he'd bought this house. The truth hit him squarely between the eyes. When he'd decided living in the rooms above Sanctum was pathetic and he'd finally started looking for a place, there had been several that had been in better locations, had nicer amenities, but he'd known he would buy this one when he'd walked into the backyard. Something had called to him, and now he realized it had been the remembrance of long nights swinging beside her. They would start out studying and end up kissing and touching and holding each other.

"Yeah."

Her hand came out, palm up. It was the sweetest offering he'd ever seen.

He slid his hand over, covering hers.

They sat there, swinging and holding hands for the longest time.

It was enough.

Chapter Five

Genny stepped off the elevator and smoothed down her skirt. It was odd to be in clothes she'd picked out herself. Brock had preferred her in fussy business suits, the same type his mother had worn. When she'd gone shopping the week before, she'd had to think about what she liked. Bright colors, tighter fits. When she'd tried to ask Wade's opinion, he'd merely said every single time that she looked lovely. She was wearing a pencil skirt and curve-hugging blouse that she was certain Brock would say made her look like a whore.

What he thought didn't matter anymore.

Ahead was a sign that read McKay-Taggart Security. Through what appeared to be heavy glass doors, she could see a reception area but it was empty. If everything went well this morning, that desk would be hers.

If she could handle it. It had been years since she'd been employed. Brock hadn't even allowed her to work at the plant. Of course, he'd pretty much been right about that. If he'd let her, she would have blown the whistle on his embezzlement practices years before. As it was, she'd only found the proof after her father died and she'd gone through his private papers. She'd gathered information for years, but it had never been enough. Her father had left behind the undeniable trail of crimes she'd needed.

"This is the main floor of the building," Wade said as he pulled out a key card. "I work downstairs, though as lean as we are in my department, they might as well move us back into the main office and rent the floor out. It's just me and Shane right now."

"I thought the company had a whole unit of bodyguards." She was nervous. Really nervous. The last week had been nothing less than fabulous. Wade had been by her side for everything. He'd sat with her and Ash when they'd met the principal of the junior high. He'd gone with them as they'd bought clothes. He'd introduced her to his friend Shane and his wife Talia. They'd had dinner one night and everything had felt so normal. He'd started to teach her self-defense techniques.

Sometimes when they were close during those sessions, she felt something physical she hadn't for years. Arousal.

She needed to remind herself that she wasn't Wade's girlfriend. She was the woman displacing him from his bedroom. She was the reason his lower back was seizing at odd times.

And it was getting harder and harder to not suggest that the bed was big enough, and it wasn't like they hadn't slept together before. She wasn't looking for sex. Except maybe she needed a reminder that sex could be good. That it could be miraculous. Or she would find out that her memory was faulty and sex was nothing special.

It was getting harder and harder.

"We had a mass exodus a couple of months back. Everyone seemed to find what they needed and moved on around the same time. Shane stayed here in Dallas. We're the last men standing since Big Tag can't seem to find anyone he's interested in hiring. My boss can be hard to take at times, but you shouldn't have to deal with him much. His wife, Charlotte, runs the actual office and she's a sweetheart. Once you learn the system, it'll be smooth sailing," he said. "Though you should be ready because sometimes things get a little crazy. If you think the office is about to get raided by a CIA team, really any armed team, you should send out a signal and then dive under the desk. Also, if you find yourself in a situation where you need to fend off an attacker with a couple of cups of coffee…well, try not to. It happened to the last receptionist. Maybe I should get you another job. Now that I think about it, this one might be dangerous."

But it was also secure. The way he'd described it, apart from the occasional misunderstanding with CIA strike forces, no one got in or out without either a key card or being buzzed in by the receptionist. She would have a monitor on her desk showing everyone coming and going. She would have control, and if something bad happened, she would also be surrounded by trained men and women who could take care of the problem. She wouldn't get that as a barista somewhere. "I think I'll be okay with this one."

A job. How sad was it that she'd once wanted to go to medical school and now she was worried she wouldn't be able to handle the phones?

Wade stopped her, putting his hands on her shoulders and looking into her eyes. "You're going to be amazing, Genny. You can do this. You can do anything."

"How can you say that?"

"Because you managed to raise that kid in an environment that was toxic. Ash could have gone a lot of ways, but you made sure he knew he was loved and had someone who would never let him down, and now he's going to thrive and you are, too." He took a deep breath. "Because I'm going to make sure that you know you're loved and you have someone who will never let you down again. If Taggart gives you hell, kick him in the balls. He'll likely stop you before you get there, but he'll respect you for trying. And if you need anything, I'm one floor down."

"You aren't on assignment?" She'd wondered because she knew his job often took him on the road. It was one of the reasons she'd hesitated to call on him.

She knew she should say something to him about the other thing he'd said. About the knowing she was loved thing, but it was easier to ignore it. It was easier to pretend she had a right to hear it.

"I'm here in Dallas for a while. Shane and I are interviewing candidates for the new team, and then more than likely one of us will always be in the office. We'll let the younger men take the long assignments. There's plenty to do here. We run a training program. Next week we've got new hires for the Loa Mali royal guard coming in. Don't worry. I'm not going anywhere."

She wished that didn't make her insanely relieved. Though she was still planning on being on her own when she could, she wasn't ready for Wade to be anywhere but at her side. "That's good to know."

He winked at her as the door unlocked. "You're going to be great. When this is done, I think we should talk about you going back to school."

"What?"

Any further conversation was interrupted by the young woman with tears in her eyes who pushed through them in her haste to get out the door.

"Are you all right?" Genny turned, watching the woman as she pressed the elevator button urgently.

She turned and shook her head. "No. He's an asshole. I have no idea why anyone would put up with him. That paycheck is not worth it."

A lovely woman with strawberry blonde hair raced up to the door. "Hey, I can talk to him. Please. I don't think the temp agency will send anyone else. I'll double the salary."

The woman simply shook her head and stepped inside the elevator.

Holy crap. What was she getting into?

"You okay, Charlotte?" Wade asked.

Charlotte's eyes narrowed as she turned. "No, I'm not. I'll be back in a minute."

When Genny turned to the office, a massive, badass-looking blond man was standing in the reception area, his arms crossed over his muscular chest. He wore black slacks and a matching black T-shirt, as though this was a man who preferred the shadows. He was extremely intimidating.

Though apparently not to the woman named Charlotte, who pointed a finger at him. "You are in so much trouble."

Wade leaned over, whispering in her ear. "That's Charlotte Taggart and her husband, Ian. This should be good. Their fights are usually extremely entertaining. The old receptionist kept a supply of popcorn for times like this."

The big guy shook his head. "She didn't pass the test. You know I'm not hiring anyone who doesn't pass the test. I'm not letting the Agency get another one past me. If Ten wanted a spy in here, I can't imagine how much that fuck Levi Green wants one. You know I would think you would be happy I'm trying to protect the office. Phoebe got past me because she did that whole 'I'm too tender and sweet for the world' thing. I went easier on her and it's not happening again."

"You're such a moron. Phoebe took all your crap because she *was* a plant. That's the third assistant you've scared off. If they run, they're clearly not Agency." It was obvious Charlotte was ready to pull out her own hair.

"I will admit there might be a few flaws in my plan, but you won't let me put the candidates all through lie detector tests and full-time surveillance for the first six months of employment," Ian replied as though that was a normal thing to say.

Charlotte's hands were fists at her sides. "You know, I would let you live in your own disorganized mayhem if it wasn't affecting the rest of us. I can't find files. You have to scan them and put them online."

"So all our enemies can hop in and read everything we've done?" Ian argued. "You won't even let me redact important information."

"Because we're not the damn US government," Charlotte argued. She took a deep breath. "Babe, I know you hate change and you've had a lot of it lately. But Alex and I can't run this company if everything is chaos. Hutch isn't Adam, but he's damn good, and you know he's going to run everything he does by Chelsea and Adam until he's totally up to speed."

"Don't tell me Adam's his backup and I'm supposed to think that solves everything. Adam did the background check on Phoebe," Ian shot back, absolutely not moving from his position at all.

"You know she's part of the family now," Charlotte pointed out.

"Part of the downstairs family," Ian replied. "When I really think about it, half my company probably doesn't walk out if Phoebe hadn't shown up. I'll do things my way from now on. You know it's only paranoia if they're not out to get you. We've got about twenty different groups from around the world who would love to get in here and gather intelligence on a certain group of men we're trying to protect."

Charlotte sighed as though she had nothing to counter that point. She turned to them. "Wade, is this your friend?"

Wade nodded. "Yes, this is Genny. We went to high school together."

"Do you believe a foreign government planted her in your hometown fifteen years ago in the hopes that she could one day maybe, maybe get a job at a company that didn't even exist back then and report back on our billing procedures?" Charlotte asked, utterly exasperated.

"I don't think so," Wade replied.

Ian pointed at him. "You don't think so but you're not one hundred percent sure."

"Do I get the doubled salary?" Genny heard herself ask. Holy crap. She hadn't even started the job and here she was asking for a raise. Who did she think she was?

She was Geneva Harris. She'd survived for years when she'd had to. She didn't have to play quiet anymore. It was time to stand up and be proud. She'd survived Brock Howard the third. She could handle Ian

Taggart.

Charlotte's eyes went wide. "Yeah. It's a more complex job than receptionist, but I can still get a temp to fill in on that job. You would do it? You would be Ian's assistant? He can be obnoxious."

Ian had a mulish expression on his face as though he was already planning on how to get rid of her.

Well, she wouldn't be gotten rid of easily. She needed this job and the benefits that went with it. "I can handle obnoxious."

"I think she should answer the phones," Wade began, his eyes wide. "It's way more relaxing. You haven't actually worked in years. Maybe we should start slow."

"Double the pay and you get to start with three paid weeks off a year instead of the normal two." Charlotte was looking at her. "And your benefits start immediately, not in six weeks."

"I get two hours for lunch every day, but I still leave at five." Was she negotiating?

Charlotte put a hand out. "You'll need it. Done. I'll start your paperwork right away. Let me show you to your office. Well, it's a cubicle, but it's larger than the others and pretty comfy if you ask me."

She had an office? "Okay."

She had an office. Holy crap. She was making twice what she'd thought she would, had all kinds of benefits, and all she had to do was put up with a bully? Bring it on.

A light happiness bubbled up inside her. It had been years since she'd stood up for herself. Hell, maybe she never really had. But she was worth this. She could do this.

"Genny?" Wade said her name like he was totally unsure this was a good idea.

She gave him a thumbs-up. "I'm good, babe." She shouldn't have said that. "I mean, I can handle this, Wade. Thanks for the chance, Mrs. Taggart."

"Do I get a say in this?" Ian asked.

"No," she managed to say in precise time with Charlotte.

Ian frowned. "We'll see about that. You know I might be older but I'm more obnoxious than ever."

Charlotte's hand came up, flipping her husband off.

Genny followed Charlotte down the hall, eager to start her new job.

* * * *

Wade turned on his boss. "I swear to god if you put her through hell, I'll come after you myself."

Big Tag watched as the women strode down the hallway toward his office. "Is that the one you told me about? The one who saved your ass?"

"The one my family used to save their asses," Wade shot back.

"Adam called. He's got an assessment for you," Big Tag said.

"An assessment?" His stomach dropped. "Ian, I can't afford Adam."

Big Tag put a hand on his shoulder. "I asked for it. You care about this woman. You need to know everything. She likely won't tell you all of it. Pride and shit. I don't care about her pride. I care about making sure her asshole ex doesn't get his hands on her or her kid. I think you'll find Adam is charging you the friends and family rate."

The friends and family rate was zero. His boss was a massive ass, but he was also one of the most generous human beings Wade had ever met. "Thank you."

"I don't like thinking about young women being used. I never liked it, but now that I have girls, I really can't stand it. Are you sure I can't murder your brother?"

Oh, he'd thought about it. "Genny would be mad."

Big Tag shook his head. "Women. I don't get them. Don't they understand how much better we would feel if we were allowed to slaughter our enemies and wear their entrails like jewelry? But no. Ian, you can't put out a hit on a CIA agent. Ian, don't slide a knife inside the doctor who gave you a prostate exam. No one ever lets me have any fun."

He bit back a chuckle and wondered at the doctor who would dare to check out Ian Taggart's prostate. He was a brave dude. "Thank you. I appreciate any information Adam can give me."

"Enough to help me cover up a murder?"

He thought about that one. "Are we killing Green or your doctor?"

"Can't find Green, but I swear that doc put a whole fist up there. And he didn't use enough lube. Apparently he didn't appreciate all the advice I gave him about how to do it. Getting old sucks. But I'll feel better when I've gotten some revenge."

He chuckled. His boss was always a good time. "I'm afraid you're on your own there." He backed up. He wanted that report from Adam. He'd been careful all week not to ask too many questions. He hadn't wanted to upset her more than he had to. This gave him all the information and none of the pain for Genny. "But when you're ready to go after Levi Green, I am with you, brother."

Big Tag sighed. "All right then. Go on. At least I think you'll stay here when you get your girl."

Charlotte was right. Change was hard on Big Tag. "I'm not going anywhere. I need this job. If I play my cards right, I'm going to have a family to support."

"Hey, have you been down there yet?" Big Tag asked.

Wade shook his head. "Nah, I missed out on the party they threw. I was in DC on a job."

A smile curled up Big Tag's mouth. "They let Adam decorate. Take a look at it. Maybe in lieu of murdering someone we can send the new guys a *welcome to the building* present. Think about it, man. I need a partner in crime. Alex turned old man on me."

"I'll see what I can do." The truth was he missed the pranks all the bodyguards used to play on each other. The Man Cave, as they called the bodyguard office and training facility, had been a fun place. Oh, sure sometimes one of the guys thought it was funny to rig his gym locker with flying condoms, but he'd gotten revenge for that.

He took the stairs and soon found himself standing outside of Miles-Dean, Weston and Murdoch – An Investigative Agency. The name of the firm was marked with very prestigious-looking gold plating. He pressed the button to release the door. Apparently though Adam, Jake, Simon, Chelsea, Jesse, and Phoebe had flown from the McKay-Taggart nest, they'd taken some of Big Tag's paranoia with them.

"Welcome, Wade Rycroft," a soft, odd feminine voice said. "Prepare yourself for an investigative service like none you have known. We welcome you to Miles-Dean, Weston and Murdoch, the future is in…"

The door came open and Chelsea Weston stood in the doorway, her eyes rolling. "Come on in. Adam is testing out our brand-new robot receptionist. If I could figure out where he put the damn hardware I would take an axe to it."

"Which is precisely why you'll never find her," a familiar voice said.

"You leave Tess alone. She's a remarkable piece of software."

Chelsea turned on him. "Like her creator, she's an overblown windbag. It takes her ten minutes to greet someone. The freaking delivery guy doesn't need a rundown of how magnificent we are every time he wants to bring me Kung Pao chicken. And it freaks them out when she knows their real names. I have to have lunch delivered upstairs. Oh, I throw it all up right now because someone talked me into keeping the British monarchy strong, but I want my lunch, damn it. Do you hear me, Tess? If you run the pizza guy off, I'll come into cyberspace and murder you."

"Chelsea Weston." The computerized voice came over the sound system. "Perhaps it's time for your meds. Your voice indicates an anger I can see no valid cause for. Let me play you some soothing jazz."

"Not smooth jazz! Not smooth jazz," Chelsea shouted at the ceiling.

But it came on, the sound of a saxophone being played by a man who had probably never played with an actual jazz band in his life. It was elevator music. A lot of loud elevator music.

"Darling, come along. I've got croissants for you." Simon Weston walked in, carrying a bag in his hand. "Come here, love. Don't let the robot get to you."

Adam frowned. "She's not a robot. She's an AI and I programmed her to properly speak to everyone. If she's rude, it's Chelsea's fault. Look. Hey, Tess. How are you today?"

The music stopped and a long sigh seemed to come from every wall. "I'm wonderful, Master Adam. The world is a beautiful place as long as you are in it. And have I mentioned how brilliant you are lately?"

Wade stared at Adam. "Does Serena know you have a girlfriend?"

Simon put an arm around his wife's shoulder and led her away while Adam shook his head.

"She's got some kinks to work out," Adam admitted.

"Yes, she has a thing for you." He wasn't about to let that one go. He might have some ideas for where Ian could hit Adam hard.

The whole office was gorgeous and peaceful. A massive fountain dominated one wall, the sound soothing to his ears. The lighting was dim and there were several seating spaces.

Adam held out a hand. "Anyway, welcome to Miles-Dean, Weston and Murdoch. Don't mind the Westons. They're busy procreating, and pregnancy does not make Chelsea happier. I wish like hell Simon had been able to carry that child because we're all in for another six months of hell. God, I pray Phoebe and Jesse decide to wait a while for their second because I can't handle another overly hormonal alpha female."

"Yes, you can, Master Adam. You can handle anything you like," Tess said over the speaker system. "You're the smartest Master in the world."

Adam flushed a bright red. "Yeah, I gotta fix that. Come on, man. We've got a report for you. Your girl's ex is a massive douchebag. You need to deal with that."

"It's what I'm trying to do." It was good to know that Adam could even get in trouble with electronically programmed females. He had to wonder what Hutch could do if he, say, managed to get into Adam's system and might feel like reprogramming Tess. That could be a fun day.

He followed Adam into the lushly decorated conference room. Where McKay-Taggart was comfortable but utilitarian, MDWM was luxurious. It was the anti-Ian office. Someone had spent some cash on those chairs. Wade entered, noting the big screen at one end of the conference room and the lovely marble table that dominated the room. Simon and Chelsea were already seated. Jesse and his wife, Phoebe, stood by the coffee bar, speaking quietly to each other. Jake Dean strode in behind Adam.

"How do you like the spa, Wade?" Jake asked, sliding into a seat at the end of the table. He had a tablet in his hand.

Spa was a good description. "It's very soothing. Tess seems to know who she likes."

Jake laughed. "Yeah, Serena hasn't heard her yet. I can't wait for her to meet Tess."

"I'm working on it," Adam replied, obviously embarrassed.

"She's obnoxious." Phoebe settled in, her husband taking the seat beside her. "She told me I should lose five pounds the other day and questioned the relevance of Hermione in the Harry Potter books. I will take down a bitch over my girl Hermione."

"She's got issues," Adam admitted.

"Yes, she loathes everyone except you." Jesse's eyes were narrowed on Adam.

"I wrote a protocol that allows her to grow and find her own style," Adam explained as he found a seat at the head of the table.

"Unfortunately, it turns out Tess is a bit of a misogynist and a little obsessive."

"She's actually a lot like Geneva's ex." Chelsea allowed Simon to hold a chair out for her. He couldn't tell from her slender figure that she was pregnant.

He wondered how Genny looked when she was pregnant. Even in the last week, she'd started to fill out again, her skin looking less sallow because she was being properly fed. He would bet she'd been skipping meals, preferring to feed her son. She'd had to make that choice because she'd had no money for food.

He was going to ensure that never happened again. "What have you found out? Brock was convicted of embezzling funds."

The team settled in. They specialized in missing persons and aiding the police in crimes where they had clues about a suspect but not the identity of said suspect. Adam Miles had developed a software that could discern the identity of almost anyone it could get a facial profile for.

Almost being the key word. Wade was aware they'd tried to use the software to identify the group of six men known affectionately as the Lost Boys. Hope McDonald had done an excellent job of erasing the records of the men she'd chosen for her medical tests. She'd wiped their memories and their identities from the face of the earth. He was certain that had to kill Adam. Adam had been so sure he could solve the mystery once he got his facial recognition software updated.

"Brock Howard the third," Chelsea said with a grimace. "Even his name sounds terrible. He did a good job living up to it. Phoebe and I have been gathering information about him. I take it you understand he was awful to his wife. From what I've found, this was not a happy marriage. It got worse after Brock's mother died. I think she had some kind of leash on him. When she passed, the incidents got more violent. Not that it's easy to tell. He was careful about hiding his crimes."

"Not careful enough," Adam added.

"Genny turned him in," Wade explained.

Simon looked down at his files. "Yes, we've noted that. She found the proof after her own father died. He was the family business accountant. He knew where all the bodies were buried and yet he never came forward."

"I think her father enjoyed the perks of being associated with the town's wealthiest family." He'd always known her father hadn't liked him. Her dad had been very unhappy when they'd started seeing each other. "I know he was at the meeting where they told her how things would go down. Yet he left her a clear path on how to send her husband to jail. I suspect he didn't realize how bad it would get for her and Ash. I also suspect he wasn't quite man enough to give up his cushy life to save them, but he was willing to help her out when it wouldn't cost him."

Now that he thought about it, very few people had ever sacrificed to help Genny. She was always the one who had to give something up.

"I would say that's probably accurate," Phoebe replied. "Are you sure you want to go over this?"

Wade's whole body tightened. "I know it was rough for her in an abstract sense. I want to hear everything. If I'm going to keep Genny safe, I need to know it all. Even if it hurts."

"You care about her? She's not just another client then?" Simon asked, settling in beside his wife.

"No, she was my high school girlfriend." He wasn't going to lie to anyone about their relationship. "I was planning on marrying her. She was going to join me after boot camp, but I got a Dear John letter explaining that she was leaving me to marry Brock because he could give her a better life. I bought it."

Phoebe shuffled through some of her records. "I was curious about that. From what I could find out, she had no interest in him prior to marrying him. Did you know shortly before the wedding, the Howard family bought the loan on your family ranch from the bank? That's unusual for an individual to buy a loan. Banks sell them to each other all the time, but this was what I would call a highly suspect transaction. Did they do it to gain leverage against Genny?"

Well, no one could say Phoebe Murdoch didn't know how to do her job. "Yes, she basically sold herself to the Howards so my family could keep the ranch. I didn't know it at the time or I would have stopped it. Instead I believed that stupid letter. I didn't go home for a long time and when I did, I avoided her like the plague. I'm not proud of how I treated her. That's why I need to make this right. Has Eve worked up a profile?"

Jesse slid him a file folder. "Here's a hard copy of Eve's thoughts. I'll email you a copy as well."

"Already done, Jesse," Tess said. "I've just sent the file to Mr.

Rycroft's work email."

Jesse frowned as though he still wasn't certain he liked having the walls talk to him. Wade was with him on that one. "Uhm, thanks, Tess."

"No need for thanks." The computer's tone had gone a little husky. "I merely enjoy serving. And might I add, Jesse, your workout this morning proves how much stamina you have…"

"Tess, sign off now. And stop watching the men's locker room," Adam commanded.

"But the men are pretty," she said before going silent.

A horny AI. He should have known that would be what happened when Adam was the man programming.

"Adam, if you don't get rid of her, I will," Phoebe vowed.

"Sorry," Adam replied, turning to him. "Now as to Eve's profile, she's absolutely certain that he will come back for his wife after he gets out of jail."

"I know I'm not a psychologist, but it's obvious to me that he's obsessed with her. Eve believes his obsession began in childhood. From what she learned from his records, Genny was his only friend," Jake said.

"Because her father worked for the family, they were together a lot when they were kids. I don't know what he was like when he was a little boy. I knew him as a preteen. By then he'd been shipped off to boarding school. He would only come home for summers," Wade explained.

"I managed to talk to some of the students he went to school with." Chelsea leaned forward. "He attended several boarding schools. He got kicked out a couple of times. Every time he got the boot it was for violence against another student. No one liked him. Most of the people I talked to remembered being afraid of him. They said everyone knew he was vicious, but he would squirm his way out of trouble until someone would bring the administrators undeniable proof. He's skilled at getting people in authority in his debt."

Wade was certain that was something Brock's momma had taught him. "I didn't know how many schools he'd gone through. I do know when he would come back for the summers, he tried to get as much of Genny's attention as he could. She never thought he was dangerous. I don't think she truly understood that he wanted her the way he did. In her mind they were friends and nothing more. She couldn't understand that he was twisted."

She'd been naïve. He'd been cynical. It had killed their relationship.

Jake shook his head at something he read in the file in front of him. "Did you know she filed three separate restraining orders between the time they separated and he went to jail? All three were rejected by the county judge."

How vulnerable must she have felt? She'd tried to protect herself and her son and she'd been told at least three times that she wasn't worth saving. "It doesn't surprise me. The Howards pretty much owned the county until recently. I assure you that judge owed his seat to the family. As well as the mayor and the chief of police. She wouldn't have had anyone in that town who would have helped her. Not if it meant going up against the Howards. It should be different now that the money is gone."

"But it isn't." Simon leaned forward. "I believe he's got several hundred thousand in offshore accounts. They froze his US accounts and seized his assets, but they didn't find the money his family held outside the US. I suspect Mr. Howard probably feels poor given the fact that he once had millions, but he still has enough to get out of the country and change his identity if he chooses to. And we believe he might have a backup plan."

"Backup plan?" He didn't like the sound of that. At one point he'd thought he could be happy if Brock simply disappeared and left them alone. He was starting to believe that Genny wouldn't be safe or secure unless her ex was either dead or in jail.

Chelsea set her half-eaten croissant aside. "We found out some rather disturbing information. Brock took out a five-million-dollar life insurance policy before he was convicted. Now obviously he can't cash in on that while he's in jail, but from all accounts he's been a model prisoner. There's no way he doesn't get out in the next few months."

"Maybe the next couple of weeks," Jake added. "The Club Fed he's at is known for letting white-collar criminals out early for time served and good behavior. He was in jail for a couple of months before he was sentenced. They could take that into consideration."

"But he left the country when he wasn't allowed to leave the damn county." How was Brock getting every privilege while he was locked up? It wasn't fair.

"I'm sure his lawyer will argue that he was only trying to save his business, the one that took care of his family. After all, he came back into the country. He wasn't trying to flee." Adam made it all sound reasonable. "The prisons are overcrowded these days. They like to let out nonviolent offenders."

"But he is violent." Not that there was proof. Or maybe there was. "Did you check hospital records?"

"Medical records are hard," Adam explained. "I don't like hacking medical systems unless I absolutely have to. We believe her, right? Because even if there are records, they would likely have notes in them that would describe how she got the injuries. If she'd told the doctors her husband beat her, they would have called the police."

So that was a dead end, too. "What do I do? If he's got a five-million-dollar life insurance policy out on her, I've got to expect that he's going to try to kill her. He'll want that money. Should I just shoot him on sight?"

"We're working with Mitchell." Phoebe looked at him, sympathy plain in her eyes. "We think we can make a case for a restraining order. We want to bring it to a judge here in Dallas where it's more likely to stick. If he gets out, we want to have someone meet him and explain that Genny is off limits."

"I'd like to be in on that." He would let Brock know exactly what he intended to do to him in vivid, violent detail.

"I think that's a bad idea," Adam said. "You're far too close to this and Eve is already worried that once Brock finds out his ex-wife is living with you, he could lose it. It could be what she calls an inciting incident. Read the file. While he's obsessed with his wife, he also hates you."

"We had bad blood as kids. It doesn't surprise me he would hold on to a grudge. I'll stay away, but if he comes close to her, you have to know I'm going to deal with the situation," Wade vowed.

"And if we have a restraining order in place, you'll have legal validation to do what you need to do." Jake's eyes had gone hard. "I know where you are. Adam and I had to deal with Serena's ex. We'll back you, but give us some time to set this up the right way. No one has to go to jail. I firmly believe no matter what we do, this man is going to come after her and you'll be there. When he's six feet under, she won't have to worry anymore."

Wade nodded, pushing back from the table, the profile in his hand. "Thank you for everything. I can't tell you how much I appreciate it."

Phoebe gave him a smile. "No problem. You're kind of our first client. Most of them run when Tess starts in on them. We really need a human receptionist."

Chelsea stood. She'd gone a little green. "If you'll excuse me, I have to do my morning purge. It comes before my afternoon and evening purges. I hate pregnancy. This is barbaric."

She ran out of the room.

"I'll go and let her yell at me for a while. It makes her feel better." Simon followed his wife.

"Oh, and you were wrong about one thing." Jesse was looking down at the file in front of him. "The insurance policy isn't on Genny. It's on her son."

Now he knew how Chelsea felt. A five-million-dollar policy on Ash? Brock was planning on killing his own son for cash? "I'll make sure he never collects."

He walked out of the office trying to keep control of his temper.

Chapter Six

"Hello, new girl. I hope you're here longer than the last one." An attractive young man stood over her desk, his arms on the top of her cubicle. "She seemed nice, but I could tell she wasn't going to pass Big Tag's new Phoebe protocols. I'm Hutch, by the way. Greg Hutchins, but no one calls me Greg. It was my father's name. He turned out to be a horrific douchebag, therefore I go by Hutch."

"My dad helped his boss embezzle tons of cash." Why had she said that?

Hutch nodded. "Cool. You're competitive. That's going to work in your favor. I can play this game, new girl. When I got bad grades, Dad would put me on bread and water for three to five days, depending on how bad the grade was. I was in elementary school."

Damn. But still… "My dad sold me off to an abusive asshole."

"I ran away from my super-cold stepmom at the age of sixteen," Hutch admitted. "She refused to acknowledge my existence when I got in trouble. In her defense, I had been arrested at the time. In the end, she signed away legal rights and gave me up to the Agency."

"At least you had a job," she shot back. "I had to sleep with my asshole. Were you forced to sleep with your captors?"

He frowned. "Nah, Ten didn't swing that way, but he did make me run laps. Want some licorice? Pops never let me have sugar so now I'm kind of addicted."

"I didn't get sugar or fat or soda. I don't suppose you have any chocolate." She wasn't a big licorice fan.

He huffed. "Are you kidding? I wouldn't be caught dead without chocolate. Maybe you want a kiss."

His voice had gone deep on the last sentence. Was he flirting with her? She was fairly certain he was younger than she was. "I think I'll pass on the kiss." And she caught on to the joke. "Unless it's covered in foil. I'll take two of those and an explanation of who Phoebe was and why I've been punished because of her all day."

Hutch nodded. "Phoebe was a CIA operative who worked here at McKay-Taggart for years undercover."

She could totally understand that. "Because the CIA wanted to make sure Mr. Taggart wasn't some kind of nut job serial killer? I could believe that."

He chuckled, a low sound that made her definitely think he was flirting. "Nah, though I'm pretty sure at one point in Tag's life, murder was on his list of hobbies. He tries not to kill anyone around his kids. Phoebe was here to watch and report on the company itself, but Jesse Murdoch in particular. Big Tag finds out she's not what she seemed, calls Ten who was her CIA handler and says he's going to take care of it. What Big Tag doesn't know is Phoebe was Ten's sister and Ten flipped his shit. I know because I was CIA at the time and got to see said shit flipping. Needless to say he used some words I don't think anyone should use, especially not when they're said with a slow Southern accent. We end up raiding the office, and who would have guessed that they were having a baby shower. Yeah, we pointed the big guns at babies. Not my proudest moment. That's why you're going to catch hell. Big Tag's got it in his head that the Agency is going to try to plant another operative, and if he's obnoxious enough he can figure out who it is."

"I'm not a CIA agent."

"That's exactly what you would say if you were a CIA agent. I should know. I took the training classes. Rule number one is to say you are definitely not a CIA agent."

She had to laugh at that. She turned and fed another document into the scanner. "Okay. How do I prove to him I'm not here to spy?"

When she looked up Hutch had completely disappeared. But she wasn't alone. Her boss occupied the entrance to her cubicle, his massive body damn near blocking out the light. He was frowning and holding a file folder.

"You want to explain to me why you've completely screwed up my filing system?" His deep voice nearly sent her into a panic.

"I…uhm, well, I thought it made more sense to file it alphabetically, sir."

"It doesn't make sense to me. I liked it the other way. Put it back."

She took a deep breath and was about to nod when she remembered what Wade had told her. If she didn't start standing up for herself, she would always be this person—good and kind and marginalized. It wasn't fair that the world was a fight, but it was true, and she had to deal with it. She could be strong or she could let asshole men walk all over her.

"No."

A brow rose over his eyes. "Excuse me?"

She stood up, going toe to toe with the man. Sure he had a foot and a half on her, but she wasn't going to let that stop her. It was time. She could make her stand and she would either get the relationship with her boss she wanted or she would find another job. No more compromise. No more getting through the day simply to survive. She wanted more out of life and she would never get it if she didn't take it for herself. "I said no. Do you know why I redid your client files? Because the way you have them is ridiculous."

His eyes went steely. "I had them in the order in which I worked them. They were timeline proper."

"I don't know your timeline. No one who is going to need those files knows your timeline. And some of them overlap. Some clients have hired you more than once."

He glared at her like she'd made his point for him. "That's why they have two files."

"Which is redundant and silly because what happens if the person who retrieves the file doesn't know you're an OCD crazy person who's a slave to the timeline? Alphabetic is the only way to go. And in the meantime, I'm going to rename every file so it corresponds to the actual name of the client or person of interest. Crazy Doctor Lady Erin Murdered is not a proper file name. Neither is Douchebag Collective Agent My Wife Blew Up." She was going now, gaining some real steam. "And while we're at it, you know for a dude who plays the badass, you have a lot of women saving people in here."

Taggart's eyes never left hers. "Did you not see the file marked Asshole Russian Mobster I Knifed? And for your information, I'm planning several future murders. Those files are coded in pink. Because they haven't gone to red yet."

He was insane. "I think all future murders should be in a different place. Maybe all files with future murder plans should be kept in a more secure location so you don't tip off the people you're planning to murder. Have you thought of that? No. You were too busy trying to figure out how to get rid of the new girl. Well, guess what? I need this job. You will get rid of me in a body bag, and I promise I won't go down as easy as that asshole Russian mob guy. I will bleed all over your precious carpet and when I'm gone, I'm coming back as a ghost and I will make your life miserable. I will wake you up from every nap. You know how you spend like an hour in the bathroom every morning? Yeah, I already know all about that. My ghost is going to make bathroom time unbearable. You'll crap as fast as you can so you can get away from me. Do I make myself clear?"

His eyes narrowed, and she was sure she was going to get kicked out. Wade would be upset with her. She would have to find another job. It would be totally worth it because she wasn't putting up with assholes anymore.

And then he smiled, a glorious expression that lit up his face and made him seem younger. "You're totally mean. I like you. You know it's wrong to threaten to disrupt a man's bathroom time. I've got three kids and a dog. None of them respect my privacy. This office is the only place where I get to be alone."

Then there was room for negotiation. "Good, then I promise to be a Valkyrie guarding the bathroom door when you need me to. That is sacred time and space and I will defend it from children, wives, and encroaching CIA special ops teams, and in exchange, I get to make these files something a sane person can understand."

He seemed to think about it for a moment. "Okay. I'm starting to see the pros of having an assistant."

There was more she wanted. "And I get to read them. Not because I'm CIA but because I'm bored and I honestly want to know how your wife blew up that dude."

He nodded. "It was cool. His parts went all over the Arabian Sea. I like to think about him in the bowels of some shark. Deal. And if I ever find out you're a CIA plant, I get to kill you and you don't come back as a ghost."

She held her hand out. "I think I can safely make that bargain."

He shook her hand. "Welcome to the team, Harris."

"Are you serious? We get to keep her?" Charlotte Taggart was standing a few feet away, an expectant look in her eyes. "Sorry to interrupt. Hutch came and told me you were about to get rid of another one."

So that's where Hutch had gone.

Taggart let go of her hand and held one out to his wife. "This one claims she'll come back as a ghost if I murder her. She's rude and called me a moron. She's perfect. I also think she's a little bloodthirsty. She's going to fit in. Now, Harris, I'm going to need you to do that Valkyrie thing we were talking about."

"You're going to enjoy some afternoon bathroom time?" It was weird, but she was going with it.

He tugged on his wife's hand. "There's probably going to be anal involved, so I think it should count."

"Ian," Charlotte said, but she was laughing.

He handed Genny the file in his hand. "You can file this one, too. Seriously, no one gets in this office."

She took the folder. "I'll make sure of it."

He disappeared with his wife. She watched as the blinds closed and heard the lock click into place.

Hutch popped up over the cubicle wall. "Dude, you handled him perfectly. So, what were we talking about?" He winked. "I think it was kisses."

She rolled her eyes and laughed as she sank down to her chair. She glanced at the folder in her hand and suddenly kind of loved her new boss.

Dick Who Hurt Wade's Chick And Is Going To Die

It was coded pink.

She sniffled a little because she might have finally found a place where she belonged.

* * * *

Wade stepped out into the parking garage. He wished he could do what he wanted to do and hold the door open for her, but he had to start adjusting her to the protocols they would use whenever they went out. "Sorry. I should go first."

She had a grin on her face. It had been there since the moment he'd stopped at her cubicle and found her flirting with Hutch. "It's cool. I suspect it's some kind of protection thing."

"Protocol," he corrected. He wasn't grinning. He was kind of sick to his stomach because she'd seemed incredibly happy talking to the younger man. Hutch was goofy, but he supposed he could see the appeal. Hutch was open and funny, and he'd never left her behind to be tortured because he was too self-involved to see his girlfriend was trying to save him.

He might be jealous. Heinously jealous.

"Protocol." She seemed to consider the word. "I like it. It sounds very professional."

"I am professional. I've been doing this for years now. I can protect you. You know Hutch is really only good with computers." And Hutch was a pilot, but he wasn't going to mention that. Nor would he mention that Hutch had been key to one of McKay-Taggart's most dangerous and celebrated operations. When he thought about it, the kid was kind of a badass.

She stopped in the middle of the parking garage. It was later than he usually left, but she'd wanted to stay behind and finish her first round of files. Apparently Tag had some meeting that kept her out of his office most of the afternoon. Wade didn't see why that meant Genny had to stay late, but she was so enthusiastic about it, he hadn't complained.

Nope. He'd sat and stewed about Hutch.

"Hutch?" She was standing there staring at him.

He jogged back to her, glancing around to make sure they were alone. "Hey, another part of protocol is staying with me at all times. It's okay when you're inside the office. Consider it a safe zone, but if we're walking out in the open, I need you to be fully aware of your surroundings. We've still got a few weeks, but I've got to get you ready for when Brock gets out. Now come on. We've got a lot to talk about."

He took her hand, happy when her fingers curled around his. At least she was following his lead. He strode to his big truck and opened the passenger side door. He could be a gentleman in this case. He helped her up.

"There's no reason for you to be jealous of Hutch. He gave me a few kisses, that's all."

He dropped her hand, turned, and started back toward the office. Hutch's truck was still here. He would kill the little fucker and that would teach him. He would torture him first. Hutch liked computers. Wade would see how much he liked them when they were shoved hard up his ass.

"Wade." Genny ran after him, her laughter a musical sound he didn't want to hear right now. "Wade, come on. I was joking. He let me raid his desk for chocolate. Those kind of kisses. Please don't murder him."

He stopped, completely embarrassed. He hadn't been thinking. She was used to being around a man who took out his temper on her. "I'm sorry. I didn't mean to scare you."

She grinned up at him, her hand on his arm. "You didn't scare me. Why would you… Wade, I know you're not Brock. I've always known that. I'm not terrified of all men. Hell, I'm not afraid of Big Tag. He's kind of funny once you let him know where the boundaries are."

"You gave Tag boundaries?" He'd been afraid to leave her alone with Ian. Not because he thought Ian would hurt her, but because he could be intimidating at times. Now that he thought about it, Big Tag was actually perfect for Genny to start practicing her newfound sass on because he would like her more if she gave him hell.

"Very firm ones, but I also offered him something in exchange. We're going to get along fine, Tag and I. And Hutch and I are only ever going to be friends. He talks way too much about *Game of Thrones*, but he does have a lot of candy so it evens out to a nice friendship." She moved her hand up to his shoulder. "I'm not interested in Hutch, but there is this guy who works in the office I am interested in."

His whole body went on full alert. He had things to tell her, things that were important, but was here really the place to do that? Here was the place to talk about work things and who she was interested in. Interested in seeing? Interested in spending more time with? "Who might that be?"

Her eyes met his, heating up. "He's in the bodyguard unit and he told me once that if I ever want a real kiss, I should ask him."

He could feel the erection coming on like a runaway locomotive. He'd spent the last few months going without. The scene at Sanctum had gotten boring for him. At first it had been filled with excitement, but watching all his friends settle down had made him look at his life in a different way. Having Genny back in it made him absolutely sure he didn't want casual sex. He wanted a woman who belonged to him, who he belonged to. He wanted disgusting, nasty, utterly committed sex. "Then you should definitely ask."

"Wade, will you kiss me?"

She looked sweet with her head tilted up and that look of expectation in her eyes. It struck him suddenly that he'd kissed a lot of women since the last time he'd kissed her and she'd only kissed one man, and that hadn't been of her own free will. He'd been the first boy she'd kissed. She'd been shy and hadn't dated much in high school. Her father had insisted she study and kept her on a tight curfew. He'd been wild while she'd studied hard.

He'd cost her everything.

"I don't know that I have a right to." It physically hurt to step back, but he didn't feel worthy of her. "Come on. I should get you home. Ash will be waiting."

His boots rang along the concrete in the otherwise silent garage. He walked toward the truck again. He stopped when he didn't hear her heels echoing. When he looked back, she was standing there again, staring at him.

Damn it. She was probably going to cry. He'd hurt her when he was trying hard not to. How did he explain this to her?

He stood there like an idiot, his hand on her door waiting for her. "Genny, come on. Let's talk."

She was still for a moment and then her heels made an angry staccato sound along the concrete. "I think we've talked long enough. Do you remember when I mentioned you owed me? I was talking about more than protection. Do you have any idea how long it's been since I had an orgasm? Well, if you're not supplying them, buddy, we should stop at a toy shop on the way home. I'm going to need a vibrator."

She ignored his hand and hauled herself up into the truck.

Damn it. "I'm sorry."

She looked straight ahead. "It's okay. I'm sorry I said anything. I thought you were still attracted to me. I would like to know something, though. Is it because I've aged or because you don't want to touch anything Brock touched?"

His stomach took a deep dive. "God, no, Genny. Nothing like that. I want you so bad but when you looked up at me all I could think of was the fact that I'm the only man you've ever really kissed, and I didn't deserve it then. I don't know that I deserve you now. I want to go back.

I want to be yours and to have only ever been yours. When you looked up at me, I had a flash of where we should be. Ash would have been our first kid but not our last. We would have raised our kids on Army bases and then come back here. We would be an old married couple, but I would still want to hold your hand because I would have forgotten what it felt like to be without you. I wouldn't be a thirty-three-year-old man who never had a real relationship because he let the only woman he ever loved go. I wouldn't ache every day with this hole inside because we didn't get that life."

She turned to him, her eyes softening. She twisted around so she was sideways in the seat, her legs hanging out of the cab, but she was able to look him in the eyes. "You have to let that go. I did a long time ago. Maybe it was easier because I had a reason to."

He knew what that reason was. "You had Ash."

"He wouldn't have been ours. He's unique and only comes from one moment in time, from one random second that produced him. I hate Brock, but you should know that I would do it all again because I would never want a world without Ash in it." Tears filled her eyes. "Wade, you can pull away from me because you think it won't work. You can do it because you don't feel that way about me. I can accept both of those reasons, but not because you feel guilty, not because you think I'm expecting the boy you were. And don't rewrite history. That boy was good to me. He showed me how good lovemaking could be. He's the reason I'm not afraid today. He's the reason I knew none of what I went through was normal. He was one of the reasons I survived. I will honor the kids we were, but I don't need to be them again. You should kiss me if you're interested in the woman I am today, because damn, I want the man you are."

Something deep inside welled up. He wasn't sure what to call it—passion, love, hope. They were all in there, but it was more. It was the desperate need to connect with her again. It pushed him past guilt, past sorrow. He cupped her face, looking at her without that terrible debt between them. What if they could move forward without the past weighing them down? He stared at her for a moment, taking in the years that had passed. They showed in the gentle lines of her face, the slight creases around her mouth. They also showed in the strength in her gaze. He'd loved the girl she'd been, gentle and smart and kind. He didn't even have words for what the woman made him feel. "You are more beautiful than anything I've ever seen. Anything."

She was more beautiful than she'd been before. She'd survived and she was going to thrive.

He lowered his mouth to hers, connecting them for the first time in years.

Their first kiss had been awkward. He'd leaned over as they'd sat on the porch swing and brushed his lips over her mouth. Well, that's what he'd intended to do, but she'd moved and he'd ended up kind of licking her chin. They'd laughed and tried again.

They needed no second try this time. His mouth came down on hers and a flash fire started in his system. He kissed her and his brain damn near shut down. All that mattered was the feel of her. How soft her lips were. The feel of her arms going around his neck. The slow drag of her tongue across his bottom lip. God, when was the last time he'd wanted a woman the way he did this one?

He knew the answer. Fifteen years ago. But this was here and now and they were in a parking garage, and fuck it all, he didn't care.

He deepened the kiss, letting his tongue play with hers. There was nothing tentative about her kiss. She was all in, her body brushing his as she twisted in the seat.

He let his hands roam, learning her curves again.

"God, I missed this. I dreamed about this," she whispered when he let her breathe.

He didn't need to breathe. She was his oxygen. He let his hands find her hips and shifted her, bringing them chest to chest. She tried to get her legs around him, but the skirt was too tight.

He'd thought about that damn skirt all day. It hugged her, showed off her hips and that luscious ass of hers. He kissed her again and again and it wasn't enough.

"Baby, let me get you home."

She shook her head as her hands found the bottom of his shirt and pulled it free of his jeans. "No. Ash is home and he would know what we're doing. I would never hear the end of it."

God, he had an impressionable teen in his home now. He had to start thinking. "All right. I'll find us a motel."

He could do that. Lots of dudes with massive erections walked up to the front desk and begged for rooms.

"Motels are for boring people. I want to do it here. Now. I need you, Wade. Everyone's gone."

He was pretty sure there were still a bunch of cars in the garage, but there weren't any close to his truck. He thought Hutch was still here and most of the crew from Miles and Dean, but he couldn't be sure because he'd just gotten a hand on her breast. Soft breast. It had the sweetest pink nipple that got tight when he sucked on it. Her breasts were exquisitely sensitive. She shivered as though she knew exactly what he was thinking.

"Baby, we can't make love in a truck."

"We did it many times in the past." Her fingers worked the buckle of his belt.

They had. Although the truck had been a beat-up piece of crap handed down from his oldest brother and shared between Wade and Heath. They'd gone to a party at a friend's house and then stopped by the lake to talk, and talking had led to kissing and kissing led to him making love to her in the cramped back seat of the cab.

At least he had some room in this sucker. And he didn't have to climb over the seats.

Were they really going to do it in the parking garage?

Her hand cupped his cock and the answer was clear. They were definitely doing it here and now. Still. "Are you sure? I want this to be good for you. I want everything to be good for you."

She stroked him, her soft palm making him struggle to breathe. "Wade, I haven't had an orgasm in fifteen years."

He gritted his teeth. He couldn't argue with that. "Then you've got time to make up. But, baby, if you want me to be able to actually use that, you gotta stop. I'm going to come in your hand in a minute or so. It's been a long time for me, too."

Not compared to her, but he wasn't a complete manwhore like some of his friends. Every stroke of her hand was pure pleasure. His cock was ready to explode. It was also ready to get inside her, and he needed to give her more.

She brought her hand out of his pants, and despite the fact that he'd told her to do it, he mourned the loss. "Get in the truck."

He practically growled at her. "Damn it, Genny. I need you to understand something. I'm going to do this for you. You seem to need something, to be in control, but that's not always how it's going to be. We need to talk about this tonight. We need to talk about some of the things I've done in the last fifteen years."

"Like gotten into whips and chains?" She hopped out of the truck, her face flushed. "I totally went through your closet. You have a lot of lube. Why is it flavored? I would think cherry or grape would be better than ginger, but it's an interesting choice. Are you the one who uses the whip or did you find out you liked getting your ass beat? I'm cool with either way, though I don't know how much I want to get paddled. The tying-up thing might be fun. But right now I'm running on a high, babe, and I want to ride your dick, so could you please lie down and let me use you? I'll tell you how pretty you are later. I stole a condom out of the kit because I wanted to be ready."

She was going to kill him. He climbed into the truck and was grateful he'd spent way too much on the fucker. It was massive, way bigger than he needed in the city, but he'd always wanted one. "We're going to have a very long talk, baby. And you might get acquainted with the ginger lube."

He lay back, pressing the button that leaned the seat back. His whole body was singing and she hadn't exactly said finding his kit had scared her. She might never want to play in certain ways, but he could deal with that. He could deal with almost anything as long as she was willing to give him another chance.

He shoved his jeans down and unleashed his cock.

She joined him, pulling up her skirt.

Was she not wearing underwear? He took the condom from her and tore it open as she managed to get the door closed. With shaking hands, he pulled it on, stroking it over his cock. "Baby, I need to get you ready."

She shook her head. Now that they were closed in together, he could feel the heat of her body, the intimacy so much greater since she'd shut out the world. "Touch me and tell me I'm not ready. I might not have been a week ago, but now it's all I can think about. I've wanted this since the moment I saw you again. Even when you were being a massive ass to me, I wanted you. I've never been able to not want you."

She was gorgeous, her face flushed with need. He shoved her skirt up higher until it was almost around her waist. He could see the hint of her pussy, and it sent his heart rate into overdrive. "I like your choice of undergarments."

"I was too embarrassed to buy them around you."

"You don't need them." He liked the idea of her walking around ready for him. Only him. God, she'd only ever willfully been with him. She was basically still inexperienced. She might be experimenting with him because he was safe. It would kill him, but he wasn't going to stop her. If this was some form of revenge, he was going to turn it around on her. He would make it so fucking good, she would never want to leave him. He moved his hand between then, letting his fingers brush against her pussy.

And then his cock was twitching again because she was right. She didn't need much more. Her pussy was wet and ripe. Her pussy was begging for him.

He intended to give it to her.

He slid his thumb up and found her clitoris. He watched as her eyes widened. That breathy gasp that came from her throat was one of the sweetest sounds he'd ever heard. His eyes met hers as he pressed on her clit and let a finger work its way into her pussy. She was hot and tight and was going to feel right when she mounted him. Her hips started to roll, finding a rhythm as he curled his finger deep inside her. He stopped abruptly, offering her his cock instead. "I want to go together. I want you to come around my cock. Ride me, baby."

She moved up, positioning herself over his erection. He gritted his teeth as she began a slow slide down his cock. Heat threatened to overwhelm him. This was what he'd wanted for years, what had been missing. Even as he'd pretended and lied to himself, he'd needed her.

She lowered herself steadily down, every inch she took making him sweat. She was tight, a damn vise around his cock. He steadied her, his hands on her hips.

"You're killing me."

Her lips curled up. "Then it's a good way to go. I forgot how big your dick is." Her head fell back as she slid those crucial last few inches. "I missed this."

"I missed you more than you know." He was going to die if she didn't move soon, but he needed her to understand. "I missed more than your body. No one ever loved me the way you did, Genny. And I never loved anyone else."

She shook her head. "I can't do that with you. Not now. But I do need this."

She shifted her hips and his eyes rolled to the back of his head, the feeling perfectly exquisite. She rolled against him and he let it go. He wasn't going to stop telling her he loved her. He would never stop that, but he was going to be with her for weeks at least, maybe months. He would win her over by giving her everything he had.

Genny rode him hard, leaning over and allowing her mouth to find his. His tongue slid against hers as his cock pulsed inside her. He wanted her naked next time, wanted every inch of her body against his, but it was too urgent. It had been too long and she needed this. It was like releasing a pressure valve to normalize.

He shoved up, forcing himself deep inside her, and he felt the moment her pussy clamped down around him, milking him for everything he had. He went over the edge a second after she did, pumping up into her and praying the moment could last forever.

Peace filled him as she slumped over, her head finding the crook of his neck.

His body felt warm and relaxed, finally in the place it needed to be.

A knock on the window had him reaching for his gun. Which was in his duffel. Damn it. Genny gasped and sat straight up.

Hutch was smiling in the window. "Hey, guys. If you're finished, I was thinking we could go get a beer."

He stared at Hutch as Genny frantically tried to get her skirt to cover her pink parts.

Hutch backed up. "No? Okay. Maybe later. See you tomorrow. And that truck's got some serious shocks on it. Way to go, Rycroft."

She gave up and buried her face against his chest. "I can't believe I did that. Is everyone going to know?"

He took a deep breath, loving the way his truck now smelled. Like her. Like sex. "Yep. The good news is no one will care. Welcome to McKay-Taggart, baby."

She was going to fit right in here.

Chapter Seven

Genny allowed Wade to help her down from her seat in the truck. She had to admit that this particular truck was way more comfy than the last one she'd made love in. And the man was even hotter than the boy.

Of course she hadn't gotten caught by a coworker back then.

He grinned at her. "Kiss me before we go in and have to pretend you didn't rock my world an hour ago."

Because Ash was home. Wade had left work and gone to pick him up from school, escorted him home, and made sure Ash was inside and secure before he'd gone back to work. That was how the man had spent his lunch break. Then he'd been willing to let her have her wicked way with him.

She was in danger with him. It would be a stupid thing to fall for this man a second time. She couldn't stay here forever. At some point she had to stand on her own two feet.

Still, she went up on her toes and brushed her lips against his in a sweet kiss. Her body reacted immediately. Years she'd gone without. Her body had been a useless thing, but now it seemed to come alive every time she saw him.

And she definitely wanted to ask him about that bag she'd snooped around in. It was in his closet on the floor with his athletic shoes and boots. She hadn't been able to help herself. It had been a little peek. And then she'd gone through the whole thing. At the time she'd kind of wanted to see what she could find out about him without asking him. It hadn't been fair, but she'd been through too much to let herself and Ash stay with a man who might be doing something he shouldn't.

Oddly, the floggers and rope and lube hadn't scared her. Even back when they were young adults, Wade had liked to be in control. Now, thanks to romance novels, she knew what to call him. Dominant. He'd always been that way. Wade was a man who liked to be in charge, who needed routine and control.

The fact that he'd taken them in and never once complained meant something. He'd allowed her needs to take over. He'd even allowed her to take control in what she thought he suspected might be their only sexual encounter.

Did he think he was sleeping on the air mattress?

Not after the day she'd had. He could sneak into bed with her after Asher went to sleep. She intended to spend all the time with Wade she could before she had to let him go. It might make things easier. They could explore what they'd missed and not wonder for the rest of their lives.

Maybe she could figure out if what he felt for her was guilt and pity.

He opened the backseat and drew out the pizza they'd picked up. "I need to talk to you about something I found out from Adam today."

She started toward the front porch. "Is he the guy who runs the other company? Ian has a bunch of wagers going about him. I had to be careful with the white board because he's got the whole office betting."

"Yeah, Adam runs a company that specializes in finding missing persons or identifying suspects in crimes. Ian thought they would be good at keeping track of Brock when he's let out of jail."

The thought sent a shiver up her spine and took some of the joy out of the day. Naturally. She couldn't do anything without Brock coming into it. "What did they find out?"

His jaw tightened and she knew whatever was about to come out of his mouth would upset her. "Were you aware that Brock took out a five-million-dollar life insurance policy on Ash?"

She stood there for a moment, allowing the words to sink in. Brock hadn't cared about Ash as anything but a tool to keep her in check. He'd spent very little time with his son unless he wanted something from her. Oh, he would force them to smile for the world's most awkward family Christmas pictures. He would use them both as props, but he didn't care about either of them. It did give her some insight into what he was planning. "He wants to take me with him, but he'll kill Ash to get the money. He likely has someplace outside the US he intends to take me to. Someplace where no one will care that he keeps me prisoner. He told me he would do it if I ever left him. He said he would find a way to get me back and he would make sure I never got away again."

The words sounded dull coming out of her mouth. She wasn't safe. It had all been a fantasy. He'd told her what he would do, and she would give him one thing—he'd never not kept his word when it came to punishment. He'd always let her know it was coming, as though he understood the anticipation was almost as bad as the pain.

"Let's go inside." Wade put a hand on her back and started gently moving her to the door.

Her feet moved, but it was like she was outside her body. He wanted to kill Ash. He was willing to murder their child in order to collect the money. How would he do it? Brock was smart. He would make it look like an accident. God only knew what kinds of connections he'd made in prison. She'd been right the first time. She had to face Brock. He wouldn't accept anything else. If she didn't, if she hid behind Wade, she would get Wade and her son killed.

She would be left with nothing but pain.

The door closed behind her and Wade strode into the small kitchen. They'd gotten a bigger table, a four top to replace the tiny bistro set. She shouldn't have made him buy new furniture. That had been selfish of her.

"Mom? How was the first day of work?" Ash popped over the back of the couch where he'd been sitting playing some video game. The couch Wade had also bought because the three of them couldn't sit on the two lounge chairs he'd had. Ash sobered when he got a good look at her. "Not good then?"

Wade moved beside her. "Ash, I need to talk to your mom."

Ash stood up. "What did he do?" He came out of the living room. "Don't tell me it's nothing. There's only one reason my mom gets that dead look on her face. It's because Brock is causing trouble. So I ask again. What did he do?"

"I think it's time we moved you," she heard herself saying. It was like she was stuck inside her body, hiding away, but that strong, unfeeling part of her had taken over. Super Mom. Super Mom felt no pain. She did what she had to do. She didn't need stupid things like a job or good sex or self-esteem. All that mattered to Super Mom was that Ash survived. Ash was the only thing Super Mom cared about. "Can this Adam person change Ash's identity?"

"What?" Ash shook his head. "I'm not changing my identity and I'm not going anywhere. We've been through this."

She turned a steely gaze on her son. "You'll do what I tell you to."

She watched as Ash seemed to grow an inch or two taller. "Not when it comes to this I don't. What's your brilliant plan, Mom? Who you going to pawn me off on? Change my name? What the fuck is that going to do?"

Anger welled and it didn't have anywhere else to go. She pointed at her son. "Stop cussing. You're thirteen years old. You don't get to talk like that and you absolutely don't talk like that to me."

He shrugged. "Hey, if you abandon me I can do whatever I like."

Wade put a hand up like he could stop them. "No one is abandoning you."

"She is. She's been waiting to do it for a long time," Ash said.

"I don't think that's what she means to do." Wade's voice was altogether too calm. "Let's sit down and talk about this."

"You stay out of it," she said. "You don't get a say in this. Although I should let you. God, if anyone knows how to abandon someone it's Wade Rycroft." The words kept coming out, hateful and hurtful, and she couldn't quite seem to stop them. It was all going to fall apart. It didn't matter how good she'd been, how much she'd suffered. One evil man wanted her and that had shaped her entire fucking life. What Brock wanted was all that mattered, and no one could help her.

She'd made the horrible mistake of being kind to him. He'd fixated on her at a young age and wouldn't let her go. No matter what she did. She'd never had a chance. A predator had gotten her scent early on, and he wouldn't stop until he devoured her. Now all she could do was try to save her son. The idea that she could have a life, a job, some love, had been ridiculous, and she had to finally learn the lesson.

Wade had paled and took a step back like she'd physically hurt him. "That's fair. But we need to sit down and talk about this. I know I…"

Ash shook his head. "It won't work. She's got her martyr face on."

Wade sent a fierce frown her son's way. "Don't talk to your mother like that. I get you're upset, son. I'm upset, but she just found out that your…that Brock took out a five-million-dollar life insurance policy on you and she's terrified."

Ash stopped. "He did what?"

She hadn't meant to tell him that. It wasn't fair. Wade wasn't Ash's dad no matter how much she…no. She wasn't going there. This was a horrible mistake. She shouldn't have come here. Shouldn't have tried.

Rage. It was all she had and she turned it on him. "You had no right to tell him that."

"But, baby, he has to know why you're upset," Wade said.

The fact that he was being understanding simply made her angrier. It wasn't fair or right, but her life hadn't been that way either. "Get your things, Ash. We're leaving."

Ash's façade crumbled, and he looked like he was five again and his father was taking his puppy away because it pissed on the floor. "Leaving? But I like it here. I don't want to leave. Mom, I'm sorry. I won't cuss."

"This isn't about you, Ash." Wade's voice sounded tortured. "Go to your room and let me handle this. I promise you this is going to be okay. You're not going anywhere. Take the pizza and watch TV and it's all going to be fine in a couple of hours. I'm going to take care of her."

"Go and get your things." She wasn't going to be taken care of. No one took care of her. They used her like her father had used her to make his life comfortable. He'd only given her a way out when it cost him nothing. Like Wade's mother and brother had used her to secure their ranch. Like her mother-in-law had used her to keep her son in line. Like Wade had used her and walked away when she'd proven inconvenient.

Years of humiliation and abuse built to something she couldn't contain. She watched as her son walked away, exchanging a look with Wade that told her he wasn't following her orders. Her son was deferring to the man in the room. The man who'd left them to fucking rot.

"I hate you."

Wade's eyes closed briefly and when he looked at her again, there was such sickening sympathy there. "You don't. You're pissed off and I'm a good target. Let it out, baby. I'm here and I can take it. Say every nasty thing in your soul and purge it out and know that I will still be standing here. I will still love you."

Love? He hadn't loved her. She'd been young and willing to please him sexually. She'd been stupid. She'd had a full ride to college and she'd picked the boy. Such a fucking moron. "I don't want your love. Your love means nothing."

"I understand why you think that, but I'm going to prove it means something this time."

Why wouldn't he fucking fight with her? The need rode her hard, much harder than even the need she'd felt to make love with him. Volcanic rage bubbled inside. Even after she'd watched them take Brock to jail, she'd kept it all inside. Habit made her push it all down, shove every emotion into some dark place, lock it up. It was only seeing Wade again that had made the chains rattle. Pulling that gun on him had been the first impulsive thing she'd done in years and years.

It had been the first time she'd allowed herself to feel anything for anyone beyond her son.

She wasn't allowed to be angry. Anger fed the beast. She couldn't cry. He didn't like it when she cried. He would give her something to cry about when she cried. He controlled everything, even her feelings. *Don't be too happy or he thinks you've done something you shouldn't. He'll take away the things that make you happy.*

"You can't prove anything to me." She pushed at him, her palms on his muscular chest. Wade had gotten a life. He'd gotten to have a career and to find friends and do normal things. Wade hadn't spent the best years of his life simply trying to survive the day. Wade had promised her a life and then lived it without her.

He stood there, his face flushed, but he didn't move to stop her. "Go on, baby. Let it go. Take it out on me. I can handle it. I want it. I want every bit of that rage. I hurt you."

Her flat palms became fists; the world was a blurry mess. When had she started crying? "You can't hurt me."

She wouldn't let him hurt her again. She didn't have feelings anymore.

"But I did," he said softly. "I hurt you. I'm so sorry I hurt you. I left you behind."

"You left me." The words came out on a strangled cry, as if she was truly facing it for the first time. He'd left her. He'd abandoned her without a thought. She'd written a letter that had been totally out of character for her and he'd bought it hook, line, and sinker. He'd never loved her.

She'd given him everything and he'd left her aching and alone. He'd left her with the monster.

"I left you." His voice was gravelly, as if he was fighting to even speak. "I left you. I knew deep down that something was wrong, but I was embarrassed. I was angry that you would even think about dumping me for that asshole. I was insecure and I bought it. Deep down I thought I wasn't good enough for you."

What he thought didn't matter. He hadn't even called, hadn't asked a single question. He'd been in another woman's bed as soon as he could. "You left me in hell."

"I left you in hell and then I didn't look back."

She wanted him to feel it. She hadn't realized how angry she was. She thought she'd buried it all, but it was there. It had festered deep inside her, ruining every good moment, taking all her hope and tainting it. Nothing good could happen to her as long as this wound was open and bleeding.

She hit him. It wasn't right or good, but she hit him with everything she had. Even as she pounded against his chest she hated herself for doing it, but then hate was kind of the point. She hated Wade. Hated Brock.

Most of all she hated herself because she'd taken it. She'd been weak. So fucking weak.

"You're not." Wade's voice cut through the screams inside her head. The screams outside. Had she been talking? "You're the strongest woman I've ever met. Even the strongest people need to let go. It's all right. Let it all out."

"Don't fucking tell me what to do." And yet she was. It wouldn't stop now that she'd busted down the door.

Every humiliation came back. Her wedding night. God, her wedding night.

Her knees hit the floor and she wondered who was crying so loudly. The sound was torn from her soul. She knew it was her but there was still distance, as if she'd done it for so long she couldn't allow herself to feel it.

She'd broken in two and the parts wouldn't go back together. Like a broken leg that hadn't set right. Sometimes the doctor had to break the leg again, reset it to enable it to heal properly this time.

She'd broken and twisted, her soul never resetting. She'd fooled herself that she was over this because she'd never let herself feel it the first time. She'd gone to a place deep inside, pretending it wasn't happening to her.

But it had. It had happened.

Wade was on the floor with her and she finally looked up at him.

It was his tears that did it. His masculine face, so stoic, always calm, was twisted with emotion. She stared at him for a moment, trying to understand. He was crying. He hadn't cried at his father's funeral and he'd loved the old man.

"Please, Genny. Please."

Please forgive him? Please don't leave him?

Please let it go. Please come back.

She screamed, the girl she'd been finally reconciling with the woman she'd been forced to become. No more Super Mom. No more Brock's fucking victim.

She felt it all, felt the fear she'd known in those first moments when she realized she was trapped. Felt the hope that Wade would see through it all and come and save her. Felt the pain…the everyday pain of being someone's punching bag.

Wade's arms went around her and she sobbed, finally able to reach for him. They'd been children playing adult games. She'd loved him. There was a part of her that still loved him. Still longed for what he could give her.

The tears came fast and furious, as did the memories. They flashed through her, all the pain finally being felt and made real so it wasn't some shadow waiting to pounce. She made it real so she could fight it, so they could fight it together.

"Mom?"

She looked up and her son was standing there, tears pouring from his eyes. Her baby. Her one good thing. She held a hand out and he hit his knees, coming into the small circle they formed. She half expected Wade to walk away, unwilling to let Ash see him like that, but he simply drew her son in, holding them both.

Like they were his family.

Like they had always been his family, merely separated for a while. Like they could mourn the years they'd lost, but they were together now and it was good and right to share their emotions.

They sat together on the floor, their tears bonding them in a way nothing else could have.

After the longest time a deep peace fell over her.

She looked at her son. "We have to make a stand."

Her son nodded. "We make a stand here."

Wade reached out, taking their hands in each of his. They sat there, connected and finally healing.

Chapter Eight

He wasn't going to sleep. He knew that. After Genny had finally broken down, they'd had dinner and Ash and she had found a movie they loved. He'd sat with them as they watched Harry and Ron and Hermione, but he felt out of place.

The pain she'd purged, he caught a lot of it, and he wasn't sure she would ever be able to forgive him.

"Can't sleep? I think it's going around." Ash sat at the kitchen table, a half-eaten sandwich in front of him.

He'd grown to love the kid. "Yeah, I'm restless. I thought I'd grab a beer. And no, you can't have one. Your mother would have my hide."

"I don't think that's the part of you she wants."

He sent Ash what he hoped was a fatherly look. "Don't get nasty."

Ash shook his head. "There isn't anything nasty about it. She loves you. It's okay when you're in love. At least that's what I've heard."

Yep, he definitely needed the beer. It was time he had a long talk with Ash and made sure he understood what was going on. "I don't think your mother loves me anymore. I think I'm what she needs for now, but she won't let herself love me again. After…well, you were there."

Ash had cried, holding onto his mom like she was a life raft. They'd been through hell together. While he'd been living his life, building a career, having fun with his friends, they'd gone through hell. He hadn't been there, had actively scorned them. They were precious and he'd worried about his pride.

"Did you know I've never seen her cry?" Ash stared at him, his gaze far steadier than a kid's should be. "I don't think she has in years.

What do you think happened tonight, Wade?"

"I think she finally felt everything and she won't be able to forget it."

His lips curled up, but the expression was bittersweet. "I don't think so. I think she finally broke through. I think she's kept it all inside. Did you know my father would punish her if she smiled too much?"

"What the hell does that mean?"

"He would lock her in a room because he was paranoid. If she was smiling too much, then she'd obviously done something she shouldn't have. I wasn't supposed to see any of this, mind you. I got very good at snooping. I found all the places where I could hear them, but they couldn't see me. I would listen because I thought someone should know what she was going through."

"Ash, I'm sorry."

He held up a hand, waving it off. "She never wanted me to know. The one time I tried to help, I ended up hurting her. I told my teacher. She was a nice woman on the edge of retirement. She went to church with my grandmother. You can imagine how that turned out. Mom told me she broke her arm because she was clumsy."

It made his blood boil. She'd been alone and the people who should have watched over her were the ones who hurt her. No one had been willing to go against the most powerful family in town. "He won't touch her again."

"I know. You'll protect her, and she believes that now. That's why she's not sending me away. But that's not what really happened here tonight." Ash leaned forward. "When I was little, I thought there were monsters under my bed. But I wouldn't look. I would lie there and I would hear things, and in my mind those creaks and scratching sounds were the monsters getting ready to attack. My mom would come in and make a big show of looking under there and finding nothing, but I wouldn't look because I knew I would see it. I knew it was there. Tonight Mom looked under the bed. She dragged it out and pulled it into the light, and it can't hurt her anymore. That monster lives in shadows. It's always waiting. If there's one thing I've learned it's that you can put the pain off, but it has to be dealt with. It has to be felt or it lingers like that monster under the bed. You think she can't forget it now. She never forgot it. She simply wouldn't look at it. She was like me, scared of what was there, unable to drag it into the light and face it."

"You can't possibly be thirteen." He was too smart, had figured out far too much about life to be some kid.

"My father wants to kill me to collect five million dollars and I wasn't even surprised. I grew up fast." Ash pushed the plate away. "Why are you still sleeping in the office?"

It was odd. The afternoon when they'd made love in the truck seemed like it had happened to a different man. Mere hours had passed but it felt like an eternity. "She hasn't invited me to sleep with her."

"But you would?"

"In a heartbeat." He probably shouldn't be talking about this with Ash, but it felt oddly normal. The house seemed fuller with Ash in it, more like this was the way it was supposed to be. As though something he couldn't explain had slid into place and the world made sense again.

"She doesn't remember what it's like to be in a good relationship," Ash said. "I think she needs you to ask. I think she needs you to put this on a normal footing. People who love each other the way you do sleep together."

"Normal sons don't try to get their mom's boyfriend to sleep with their mom."

"As we've decided, I'm not normal." Ash was quiet for a moment. "I wouldn't have said anything if you weren't the man I was talking to. I've spent a lot of time lately wondering what it would have been like if you were my dad. I know what Mom says. Mom thinks I'm this unique creature only formed in that one moment and never again or some shi…stuff. I don't think so. I think she was always going to be my mom, and if she'd been with you, you would be my dad and I would have grown up this Army brat with a couple of siblings who got into trouble and gave my mom and dad hell because we could. Because we wouldn't know how unsafe the world could be. We would live in that bubble of childhood most kids get."

"We can choose." He was constantly floored by how smart Ash was, but this was something he'd learned. "Blood doesn't make a family. I love my brothers, but I'm closer to the people I work with. I spend my holidays with them. I watch their kids grow. I depend on them more than I've ever depended on my blood family. We can choose, Ash. I love your mother. I don't want to ever let her go. I want to be your dad. We don't need an ounce of blood between us to make that true."

The kid smiled and this time it was a joyous thing. "I want to be your bratty kid. And she wants you. She looks at you like I've never seen her look at any man. Do the work. Ask her. Go knock on her door. Let her make the choice, but she should know what you want."

"You're going to kill me, kid." But he was standing up, knew what he would do next. "Don't stay up too late. You have school in the morning."

"Spoken like a true dad," Ash said with a smile.

It was time to figure out if he had any chance of giving Ash little brothers and sisters to corrupt.

* * * *

The soft knock on the door brought Genny out of her trance-like state. It was like she had to shut down to process what had happened to her. Everything that had happened to her. She'd known it all on an intellectual level, even on a physical level she had the memories, but she wasn't sure she'd accepted it in her soul. Ash was right. Deep down, she'd been waiting for that moment when she faced Brock and her pain ended one way or another. She'd been in that place for so long that she equated life with pain, but it didn't have to be that way if she was willing to open herself up. She'd closed down in an attempt to not feel the pain, but it had taken the joy, too.

She forced herself off the bed and hoped whatever Ash needed didn't take too long because she had to talk to Wade. She had to tell him she didn't want to pretend anymore. God, she didn't want to sleep alone anymore.

She opened the door and stopped because it wasn't Ash standing there. Wade was there wearing pajama bottoms and a black tank top that showed off his ridiculously muscular arms and shoulders. It molded to his body, letting her see the sculpted planes of his chest against the thin material. It reminded her that she'd made love with him but not gotten his clothes off, and that seemed a shame.

Of course, that also meant he hadn't gotten her clothes off, hadn't seen the C-section scar she sported or the way her breasts weren't as perky as they'd been when she was eighteen. God, he hadn't seen her body since it had been at the height of its perfection.

"What's going through that head of yours, baby?" Wade asked, his voice deep.

His voice had a direct line to her pussy. It was like the damn thing had been waiting to hear him again in order to wake up and shout "pay attention to me, I have needs!" "I was thinking about how long it's been since we were really together. It was silly."

Worrying about whether or not he would reject her was foolish, too. He either would or he wouldn't. She couldn't go into her shell and hide and not take the chance because her boobs might not be perky enough for Mr. Perfect.

"I wanted to see if you're all right," he said, his eyes on the floor. "It was a rough night."

Beyond rough. But it had been necessary. She'd thought she was moving, but she'd been taking baby steps, and the minute Brock intruded, she'd sprinted back to her hidey-hole. "Will you sleep with me?"

His eyes came up pretty damn fast. "I was going to ask that but I thought I should ease you into it. I…don't hate me, but I asked Ash's advice. Not like about how to seduce you but more like if he was okay with it. He was."

It was sweet to see him fumbling. She would bet he never did. And she could bet Ash approved. "You should know that he's invested in this relationship. I think he wants you to be his stepdad, and you should consider that. I can't play around, Wade."

"I'm not playing."

Ash was the wild card. Ash was the reason she shouldn't do this. "I'm not sure I'm ready to commit to anything or anyone. There's still a part of me that's angry with you. There's a part of me that might need to try this on my own once the situation with Brock is stable and it's safe for us."

"I'm willing to take that chance," he said, his voice steady. "Don't use Ash as an excuse to keep us apart while you're here. He's a smart kid. He knows nothing is certain."

"Which is precisely why I shouldn't put him in a situation that's on shaky ground."

"Are you going to cut me out of your life if you leave?"

"No. I like my job. I don't want to leave it and you work there, too." She hadn't considered it. "I don't know, but I think Ash needs stability."

"I'm stable and I'm not going anywhere. That won't change if you decide to send me back to the office tonight. I'm going to be here for you and Ash. We don't have to live together or get married for me to be willing to parent that kid with you if you'll let me. He needs a man in his life and I want to be that man. I want you and I want Ash in my life. I'll take you any way I can, even if it's only to be your friend, but you should know that I'll vet every single man you…"

She cut him off because he'd said everything she needed to hear. For a man of few words, he knew which ones to say when he needed to. She went on her toes and planted her mouth on his, loving the way she caught him mid speech and he stood there like he couldn't quite believe what was happening.

Then his hands found her waist and his lips were moving against hers. His tongue came out, rubbing and tempting as their bodies seemed to mesh. This was what she'd missed this afternoon—the feel of his body pressed against hers, the knowledge that they didn't have to hurry. They had all the time in the world to explore and enjoy.

To rediscover and relearn.

She let her hands run along the sides of his chest, dragging the tank top with them. She wanted to see him, every inch of him this time. His arms came up, helping her get rid of the shirt. He moved them inside, the door closing behind them. He only briefly stopped kissing her. It was a mere moment, but she missed him in that second. It flared inside her like something newly born. She would miss him if she left, if he left. Something precious would be lost if she didn't take a chance with him. She couldn't promise anything, but she needed to be in the now with him.

He was right. There was no reason they couldn't have this.

She was free. She'd taken herself back tonight and this was her reward. She could have him for as long as they lasted. She got to make her choices this time around and she chose him.

Of course she'd chosen him the first time around, but she'd made a terrible mistake.

"I should have been honest with you."

He shook his head, lowering his forehead to hers. "You were trying to do something right and good. But, baby, if something like this happens again, you have to treat me like I'm stupid. You have to come to me and tell me what's happening because if you walk away, I'm going to assume you've been taken and I'll fight like hell to get you back. If you really want to go, you better make sure I understand."

Because this time he would fight for her. Because this time he wouldn't let her go because of pride.

He was so beautiful. When he'd been younger, he'd been lovely. He'd played football and worked on the ranch. He'd been fit, but now his body bore the scars of his Army days, and she found it even more attractive than it had been before. It was because he'd survived. Like she had. They were older now, harder and more careworn, and still beautiful.

She placed her palms on his chest, connecting them again. His scars were old, merely pieces of the landscape now, but they told the tale. "You were wounded in combat. Is this from the firefight outside of Mosul?"

He nodded solemnly. "I'm surprised you know that."

"Your brother told me all about you. I would pretend I didn't care, but I also wouldn't let him stop."

His fingertips reached up, brushing across her cheeks and smoothing back her hair. "I couldn't stand to hear about you. Now I wish I had. You have to know that no matter how I felt about you, what I thought you'd done, I would have killed him had I known he was hurting you."

She did believe that.

He wasn't finished. "Which is why I may never be able to forgive Clint."

"I don't want any more anger. Please. Not tonight." She couldn't think about this now. She would have to find a way to mend that fence. After everything she'd gone through she wasn't about to let it wreck the very family she'd been trying to save.

"Not tonight." He leaned over and kissed her again. She never got tired of his mouth moving over hers. He dragged her up against his bare chest and she could feel her nipples getting hard and ready. She'd taken off her bra an hour before and now she hated the T-shirt between them. "Nothing but us tonight."

His hands went down to her waist and she took in a deep breath. There was no putting this off. Either he would accept her body as it was or he would reject her and she could get on with her life. He drew her T-shirt up and she could feel cool air on her breasts.

"I want to know what you do with the things in that bag of yours." She'd been thinking about it for days. Her first instinct had been to shrink back, like she'd opened Pandora's box or something. Her second had been to think about how those items she'd found—the flogger and ropes and oddly shaped plastic things she was fairly sure were supposed to go up her butt—they were tools, not bad in and of themselves. They were whatever the person using them chose. Brock would have used them to inflict pain and humiliation. How would Wade use them?

He stared down at her breasts. "We don't have to ever play like that. It's okay. I can be perfectly vanilla. I can be gentle with you."

And that was all he would ever be if she let him. His guilt would lead him to cut off part of his personality, and that wasn't what she wanted at all. She didn't want to cut herself off from exploring. "I don't need that. I want to know. Besides, what happens if I can't be gentle with you? What if I'm the one using that flogger on you? And the plug thing. I know what that is. I read, you know."

He flushed the sweetest shade of red, and suddenly she was in his arms. He hauled her up and started toward the bed. "First of all, you're not trained on that flogger so you won't be using it on anyone. Secondly, that plug is getting tossed out. If you want to play, I'll buy all new toys for you. Just for you. To answer your question, they're all sex toys. I like to play and my preferred mode of play is called Dominance and submission."

She winced. She couldn't help it. "I don't like that word."

He lowered her to the bed. "Precisely why you never have to try it."

"Stop putting words in my mouth."

"That's not what I want to put in your mouth, baby."

She rolled over, getting up on her knees. "I'm serious. I never got to experiment. I got six months of you getting on top of me as often as you could and then, well, let's simply say my sex life hasn't been fun. I want to know what other women know. What do you like about Dominance and submission?"

"D/s. You can call it that," he offered. "We talk about it being a lifestyle, but I'm more of a bedroom player, though I'm quite well trained. I have a second job. When I first came here, there wasn't much of a bodyguard unit. I ran Sanctum for Big Tag. Technically I'm still the Dom in residence."

That didn't surprise her. She'd been joking when she'd talked about Wade taking the flogger. It was obvious he would be the one wielding it. Even when he was eighteen, he'd been outrageously dominant when it came to sex. He would take control and she'd never regretted it. He'd never brought her anything but pleasure, which was precisely why she wanted to explore this with him. "What do you do as the Dom in residence?"

"Take off your undies and I'll tell you. I don't mind talking, but I want something pretty to look at. And I'm sad that you found underwear."

She wrinkled her nose. "I don't like panty lines, but I wear undies most of the time. I'm getting used to wearing fashionable clothes. I'll have to get acquainted with thongs." She felt the need to warn him. "I have a C-section scar. I don't look the way I used to."

"No, you don't. You're far more beautiful."

She would have to believe he meant that. She wasn't going to let her insecurities hold her back. She hooked her thumbs under the waistband of her undies and drew them down before tossing them away.

"Like I said, far more beautiful." Wade stared at her and there was no way to miss the bulge in his pants. His cock was long and thick and hard. His cock didn't seem to have a problem with the changes in her body. "Lie back and put your hands over your head. You want to play? I want to play. Anything that scares you, anything that doesn't turn you on, you let me know."

He disappeared inside the closet for the briefest of moments and was back with that bag she'd been thinking about. He unzipped the top and pulled out a length of rope. "I'd like to tie you up. The reason I want to do this is to help you focus on what I'm doing to you. You won't be able to move. You'll only be able to lie there and take the pleasure I'm giving you. Also, I think you'll look incredibly hot. It'll make me feel like I'm in control, and that does something for me."

Control. She always had to be in control. Not of her life. She hadn't had any of that, but she'd had to be in control of her emotions, of the expressions on her face, of every word that came from her mouth. She hadn't been able to let go in years. She allowed her arms to drift over her head, deeply aware of the fact that she was naked. Her skin felt sensitized, as though she could feel everything—the softness of the comforter under her, the cool air above. Her nipples peaked, hardening under his gaze as arousal started to wind through her system like a river that had been dammed up for far too long.

He took her wrists in his hands and started to bind her hands together. "If I scare you, tell me and I'll stop."

"I'm not afraid of you." Not physically. That was for certain, but she was scared of how much she felt for him. She didn't have to make a decision now. She could let them be for a while, but down the line they would have to figure out if they worked. They would have to find a connection that went beyond their past, beyond his guilt and her need to feel safe. They had to figure out if they could love each other in the real world.

"I don't ever want to hurt you again. I think you might like this. I think this might help you focus. When we're playing, I'm in control. When we're playing, you're all mine and your only role is to take what I give you." He tied off her hands and then bound them to the headboard of the bed.

She was caught, trapped, but it was all right. She knew she didn't have to be tied up to be helpless. This wasn't something Brock had ever done to her.

Wade stared at her. "Don't think about him."

"How can you tell?"

"I watch you. I study you. I want to know how to read your every mood so I can be a better partner to you. Sometimes you don't talk to me. I have to find other ways to know how you're feeling, what you need." He placed a hand on her chest, right between her breasts. "I know the look you get when you think about him. He has no place here. I won't let him come between us again."

She took a deep breath and let the thought go. There was only Wade tonight. "All right. You're in control."

Except she could stop him whenever she liked. His control was an illusion, "play" as he called it. She relaxed and let herself feel. His hand moved down her body, leaving a trail of heat everywhere he touched.

"The key to D/s is communication, but we can communicate in different ways. I can watch your body to see how you react, to know how a touch affects you." He palmed her breast, cupping it. She'd missed this during their afternoon quickie. She'd missed his touch. "You like this."

She let her eyes drift closed in order to concentrate on the feeling. Heat pulsed through her system. "I do. I love it when you touch me."

"If you would let me, I would never stop. I don't like sitting apart from you. I want to sit next to you, where I can touch you and feel you against me. And I was jealous of Hutch today."

That was ridiculous. "He's a child."

"He's not really," Wade replied thoughtfully. "He's been through a lot and I bet he's hiding a ton of pain under all that candy, but he's also smart and he never hurt you the way I did."

"I think you should make it up to me with sexual favors."

"I can start there. How do you like this?"

She gasped as something soft stroked over her. The feather. She'd wondered why he had a feather wrapped in plastic in the bag. It had seemed out of place with all the leather and hard plastic, but now she sighed as it floated over her skin, the soft tendrils making her shiver with pleasure. The feather trailed down her torso, making its way to her pelvis. He let it lightly stroke her. Her breath deepened as she felt her skin heat, all her focus on the sensations he was giving her.

The feather teased around her pussy and then moved on to her left leg, and then came back up her right. Frustration welled and she remembered this game well. "You did this to me before you even knew what D/s was. You're the world's worst tease, Wade Rycroft."

He chuckled as he kept up the slow play against her skin. "It's not a tease if you eventually get what you want. And even back then I knew what I had to do to keep you focused on me. I wanted to make sex last because it was the only thing I could truly give you. I would take you right to the edge and then pull back because I didn't want it to be over. For that time you were all mine and when it was done, I had to share you, and I knew I always would."

"Share me?"

"With your friends and your family. With your job at the factory. With the kids you tutored. With that big brain of yours. You were incredibly smart, and like most incredibly smart people it can take a lot to get you to turn off your brain and focus on the now. Even when I was younger I knew that. I wanted your full attention the way I do now. I didn't know what to call it then, but I was already practicing a form of D/s. Then, like now, I kept it to the bedroom. I was more than willing to follow your lead in most things, but when my mouth was on you, my cock inside you, I wasn't going to share you with anyone. Not even yourself."

She did exactly what he accused her of. Her brain was always working, had been even back then. If he hadn't forced her to concentrate, she would have thought about anything except what he was doing to her. She might have found some pleasure, but they wouldn't have connected the way they needed to. If there was one thing she remembered about Wade, it was the way he'd always looked into her eyes and pulled her into a world meant only for the two of them.

Did he look at all his lovers that way?

She forced the thought away. It was the past and she lived in the now. No past. No future. It was the only way she could be. The feather brushed against her pussy and she could barely breathe. He teased her clit, brushing it over her bare flesh, and thanked the universe one of the things she'd done the week before had been a full spa day with Wade's friend's wife, Talia, who she was already getting close to. While Shane and Wade had watched a game, she and Talia had facials and massages and a full Brazilian. At the time she'd simply done it because she'd never had one before and it seemed rebellious. Now she understood. The skin was far more sensitive than she'd imagined. There was nothing between her and the sensation her lover was trying to give her.

"Do you have any idea how much I love looking at you?"

She kept her eyes closed, concentrating on him, on the sound of his voice, the feel of his touch. "I was worried you wouldn't like the changes. I've had a baby since the last time you saw me."

"Here?"

She opened her eyes because she could barely feel what he was doing. She looked down and he was running the feather along her C-section scar. "It's not sensitive."

"No, but it's strong. It's holding you together and I honor it." He bent over and kissed the scar, moved his mouth across it so he didn't miss an inch.

She couldn't feel it, but tears pierced her eyes from the sweetness of the gesture. "I love your scars, too. I love them because they mean you're alive."

He stopped for a moment. "For a while I didn't want to be. I know you think I breezed through what happened, but I shut down. I know I went a little crazy. God, Genny, I don't know how to move on. I don't know how to forgive myself."

"I forgive you. That means you have to forgive yourself. It isn't up to you. It's up to me. I want your passion. I want your need. I don't want your guilt. Let it go. Shove it out. Like my ex, it has no place here."

The last thing she wanted was to have him make love to her out of anything but passion.

Wade's eyes were steady on her. "It's going to take time. Right now I need to hear that you want me. I need to know that this is about more than protection. I'll give that to you for free. I'll give you a place to stay and safe harbor. You don't owe me your body or your love. I wasted that. I want it more than I want my next breath, but I have to know I can give you something beyond saving you."

"I think I mentioned you owed me orgasms."

"I want to do more than owe you. I want this exchange between us to be something that never ends, that you simply expect because I'm your man."

She couldn't think that way. "Please don't make me choose now."

He went still, as though contemplating what she'd said.

"I can't think about the future yet," she explained. Even after everything that had happened today, she couldn't commit. She might never be able to again. The idea of getting married, taking that chance…no, she wasn't ready, and she knew that was what he was talking about. He would want to marry her because in his head it was the only way to get back what they'd lost. The problem was a piece of paper couldn't give them back time. It couldn't move them back fifteen years and let them start over.

"Then we should make the best use we can of the here and now." He placed the feather on the nightstand and dropped his pajama bottoms. He was gorgeous without his clothes, every line and plane of his body masculine and muscled. There was a dark look in his eyes, predatory and lustful. It did something to her, heightening her arousal and making her squirm.

"Tell me I don't have to be gentle with you." His voice had deepened. His cock was fully erect, a beast waiting to be let off the leash. "I can if you need it, but I'm not feeling gentle tonight."

Because of everything that had happened. He'd been there with her, but he hadn't found the same peace she had. This was his way of finding peace, and she wanted that for him. "I trust you. I don't need you to be gentle. I need you to be Wade."

He climbed on the bed like a tiger ready to pounce. He took her ankles in his hands and spread her legs, moving in between them. "I like you this way. You look gorgeous all tied up, and more than that, you can't run from me. I spend an enormous amount of time worrying about you running away. I want to give you something worth staying for."

Before she could protest, he leaned over and put his mouth on her pussy. She knew she should say something about staying but all that came out of her mouth was a low moan of pleasure. Heat spread from her core, moving through her system like lightning. His tongue was silky smooth against her skin.

Pleasure pierced through her as his mouth and tongue worked her over.

"Oh, god. You didn't…you never…"

He turned his face up, and she could see his lips glistening with her arousal. "I was a kid. I only thought with my dick. Genny, has no one ever eaten this sweet pussy before?"

She shook her head. The ties that bound her pulled at her body until she felt like a bowstring ready to release. "No. There was only you and then…"

"Only me." He turned back to his work, licking her in long strokes of his tongue. "I was always too impatient with you. There was never enough time. I never slept beside you or woke up with you in my arms. I want that now. Even if you leave me in the end, I want to spend whatever time we have together doing the things I should have done."

Again, something they should talk about, but he took her breath away. She rather thought he was doing it on purpose, but then she couldn't think anymore. He sucked on her clit and the bowstring was released, her body exploding with sensation.

She cried out his name, pulling against the ties around her hands as she rode the wave of the orgasm.

Then he was up and moving over her. He reached out and grabbed the condom he'd pulled out of his kit and rolled it over his cock with shaky hands. He wanted her, wanted this. It made it easier to let go and not worry about what would come from letting him in her bed. It didn't matter because she was caught, trapped, and she didn't honestly want a way out yet. Like the ties on her hands, she enjoyed the fact that she couldn't waste time fighting him. She was here and this had been inevitable.

He pressed her legs up, laying them flat against his chest while his cock began to press inside her. He was big, stretching her wide. He was manhandling her in the best way possible. This was his "control."

"You're so fucking tight like this." He growled the words. "I want you in every position imaginable. Get ready because the nights are mine. I'll do anything you like during the day, but after Ash goes to bed, you become mine. Not a mother or a wife. You're my lover, my sweet sex toy, and I'll have you in ways you never thought of."

He pressed his cock in and slowly dragged it back out, seeming to enjoy the leisurely pace he set. In and out, savoring every inch.

It was driving her crazy. Even his words seemed to send her higher and higher.

"I'll play with you every night. I'll tie you up and torture your nipples until you beg me to stop. I'll bite them and lick them and decorate them with clamps. When I'm done with your nipples, I'll concentrate on your pussy. I'll eat your pussy so often, you'll come just thinking about my mouth on you. I'll make a meal of you every fucking night."

She could be who she needed to be during the day. She could be strong and resilient, making all the choices she needed to make for herself and her son, and then at night she could let it all go. She could turn herself over to him and let him take them both someplace amazing.

It was the closest she would ever come to happiness.

He pressed her legs apart, moving her where he wanted with ease, never losing his rhythm. He pounded into her, driving his cock deep inside.

The world went spinning again, pleasure bubbling over her. She couldn't breathe for a moment, but it didn't matter as she watched Wade's gorgeous face go hard. He held himself against her, every muscle in his body going rigid, and then he collapsed on top of her. His weight pressed her into the bed. She couldn't remember the last time she'd felt warm and pleasantly lethargic. Her nights hadn't been spent sleeping peacefully, her body well used.

"Let me stay with you." He whispered the words against her neck.

She nodded her assent and worried she would never be able to let him go.

Chapter Nine

Genny reached up and grabbed the box of cereal Ash liked. Three weeks into her new life with Wade and she was enjoying the little things. Things like going to the movies and buying groceries. It was silly but she hadn't done those things in forever. Well, not when she didn't have to watch every single penny. When she'd lived in the mansion, it had been done for her. Brock would never have trusted her to properly buy groceries. After the divorce, going to the grocery store had been a study in humiliation.

Not today. Today she got to buy anything she wanted. She had a debit card and the code and yes, they were Wade's, but she was okay with that. She was cooking. Ash cleaned. Wade bought the groceries for now. She was going to help out once her paychecks started coming in next week.

She had to think about how she was going to get Wade to let her pay rent. If there was one thing she wasn't going to think about, it was moving out. She was crazy about him. But she had to consider whether or not she could give him what he needed. She'd learned a lot about the club Wade oversaw. Sanctum.

Her cell phone trilled and there he was. The handsome, amazing man who rocked her whole world and made her feel safe. "Hey, babe. Are you almost done at the club?"

She'd dropped him off at Sanctum and Ash at his new friend's house. She'd gotten her nails done and gone by Ulta, and then headed to the grocery store. Wade had to make sure the club was ready for the night's sessions and Ash was studying. Probably by playing video games and drinking root beer, but she was too happy for him to have friends to even question it. Wade hadn't even blinked when she'd asked him if she could take the truck. He'd handed over the keys and promised that soon they would look for a car for her. She needed her own.

Sweet freedom. Sweet man.

"I should be ready in about thirty minutes, but take your time. I've got everything set up, but there's some paperwork I need to get done. I was calling to make sure you found your way back to the store okay."

She loved the deep rumble of his voice. "I followed the GPS. I'm good that way."

He sighed. "I'm sorry. I worry. He was released yesterday."

"And I'm in a perfectly public place. He'll bide his time," she replied. They'd had this freak out the night before. She was calm now. They'd gone over every possible scenario. "We don't even know that he's figured out where I am. I can't live my life in hiding."

"I know, baby, but I don't like the fact that he didn't go back to Broken Bend. We're not sure where he is. Until I can tag his car and cell phone, I'm going to be on the nervous side."

"I'm surprised he didn't go back, but I would also assume he's embarrassed. I don't know who he would have called to give him a ride if he didn't have someone bring his car in."

"We're shorthanded right now or I would have had someone following him twenty-four seven," Wade admitted. "I'll get Ian to hire some new guys. I promise."

She felt different. In the days since she'd cried and held onto him, since she'd welcomed him into her bed, she felt stronger. "We can't do that. Think about this, Wade. If we start down that path, we'll be doing it forever. We have to live our lives and deal with what happens. I've thought a lot about this and I've come to a conclusion. Brock's a coward. He made sure you wouldn't be around to confront him. He was afraid of you fifteen years ago. We have to face him in court in a couple of weeks when the judge reviews our custody agreement. I think you should have a talk with him, let him know what you'll do if he doesn't behave."

Wade was silent for a moment. "I was already planning on that. I kind of thought I would have to sneak around you to do it."

She could understand that. "Nope. I'm going to let you be forthright and upfront, and we're going to hope prison changed him."

It could happen. Maybe. Perhaps he would take the hundred K he had in offshore accounts and leave her be.

And find some other woman to abuse. Yeah, that thought didn't make her feel better.

"I think I'll believe that when I see it," Wade said. "You be careful and get some toothpaste. Ash stole mine and you like that sandpaper."

She laughed. Sharing a bathroom with a man who cared about her was different. He tried to respect her space. "Will do. I'll come back to the club when I'm…"

She stopped in the middle of her sentence. Standing there in the aisle ahead of her was a tall man. He was lanky, though she was sure he thought of his slender frame as elegant. Unfortunately those slim limbs held a lot of strength, as she'd learned. He could easily break her when he wanted to, and he often wanted to.

"Baby? Did I lose you?"

Her heart pounded in her chest, making her bones ache. Her vision threatened to go black, but she managed to hold it together. "He's here."

Brock Howard the third was staring at her, his eyes dark and cold. "Is that your new boyfriend? Or should I say your old boyfriend? I should have known you had not a creative bone in your body. You should hang up on dear old Wade. We need to talk, Geneva. I won't take no for an answer. If you choose to bring him into this domestic disagreement of ours, I'll have to deal with him. You won't like how I deal with him."

Wade's voice came over her phone. "Genny? Baby, I want you to…"

She hung up. It was a habit, obeying Brock. The minute she did it, she hated herself, but in that moment she'd seen Wade dead on the floor because she hadn't been fast enough. Her chest ached, like someone had kicked her and knocked all her air out. That light happiness she'd felt had fled and left behind nothing but terror. He was here. He was here and he would take everything she loved away.

She loved her son. She loved Wade. She had to protect them both.

Brock was staring at her, his eyes narrowed and a sneer on his face. "I don't like the fact that you cut your hair. You know that wasn't allowed."

It was okay. She was in a public place. He couldn't hurt her in the middle of a grocery store. And she'd been stupid to hang up with Wade.

There was a deli at the front of the store with tables. She would go and sit and call Wade back. Her first instinct was to run, but Brock could catch her out in the parking lot and she couldn't risk that. Public. She had to stay public. "I assume divorcing you wasn't allowed either and yet here we are. You'll excuse me. I have shopping to do."

She started to turn, moving the cart in an arc. A sharp pain bit through her arm as he grasped her and hauled her back around.

"Don't you think you can walk away from me, bitch."

She glanced around to see if anyone could help her. A woman was at the end of the aisle. She had gray hair and stopped for a moment, but she took one look at what was going on and turned away, hurrying back toward the dairy aisle. No help from that quarter. "You're hurting me."

"Yeah, well, you sent me to jail. This is the least of what I plan to do to you. Now here's how this is going to go," he said, every word a bullet from his mouth. "You're going to walk out of here with me and we'll go get our son. We're going to Houston. We'll start over. You'll be a good girl or you'll suffer the consequences."

She tried to pull away from him. "Let me go. You don't want to start a fight here."

He chuckled. "I'll start a fight anywhere I please. You think anyone will believe you? We were married for fifteen years. It's well known how good a husband I was and how vindictive you are. Why do you think no judge would give you a restraining order?"

"Because you paid them all off one way or another. You can't do that now, asshole."

His grip tightened. If he twisted just the right way, he might break her arm. "Watch me. I've got people lined up who are going to talk about how I took the fall to keep you out of jail. They'll testify that you're a horrible mother and you've taken my son into places children shouldn't go. Do you know what your boyfriend is into? Do you know what happens at that club he runs? No judge is going to let you keep our son living with that fucking pervert. And when I have him, I'll have you, right? Or has your pussy overridden your motherly instincts and you're ready to throw the brat out for Wade fucking Rycroft?"

Brat? She hated it when he called Ash a brat. He did it because he knew it bugged her and she'd learned not to respond, but the other night had happened. The wound had been reopened and purged and she could feel again. She could feel rage. Genny picked up the steel can of pineapple juice she'd put in the front of the cart next to her purse. She'd gotten it because she wanted to make piña coladas and sit in the hot tub when Ash stayed the night at his friend's house. That was blown now. Wade wouldn't let Ash out of his sight, and she could freely use the can to bash in her ex's head.

She brought it up and back, ignoring the pain in the arm he was holding.

You have to concentrate. Ignore everything but the goal. Get him to back off. Get your space and then you can deal with everything else.

Wade's words were in her head. Despite the fact that he was miles away, he was here with her. He was whispering in her ear, telling her what to do and that she was good enough to do it.

The can met Brock's head with a satisfying *thunk*. He groaned and released her arm. A thin trickle of blood showed up on his forehead and Genny heard a gasp from someone who had been walking down the aisle. She barely had a glimpse of someone turning and running but she couldn't think about that now. She was reaching into her bag and pulling out the mace she'd bought months before. She sprayed it toward Brock, who slapped out at her.

Genny turned and ran, leaving her cart behind. It didn't matter. She wouldn't be going out to get groceries again. Brock had ruined everything. She'd been a fool to think he might have changed.

She started to run toward the front of the store. She had to get away. All her plans were gone, her good sense overridden. Panic threatened to overwhelm her. This couldn't happen to her again, not after everything she'd gone through. If he got his hands on her, her life would be over.

She was almost to the exit when a man stepped in front of the doors. He was wearing a short-sleeved shirt, tie, and khakis.

"Stop," he said and he was joined by two young men, blocking her path. They looked to be cashiers or stock boys.

"My eyes." Brock stumbled behind her.

"I called the cops." The man who'd fled from the aisle stood off to the side, his cell phone in hand. "I was there. I saw everything. She went crazy on him. She could have killed him."

The cops. They'd called the cops? That was good. The cops…would likely listen to the man who'd said she'd gone crazy. He hadn't heard what Brock had said to her. He hadn't seen Brock gripping her arm.

"She's my ex-wife. She hates me. I wanted to talk about our son. She won't let me see him. Now she's trying to kill me," Brock managed as one of the employees gave him a bottle of water to douse his eyes with.

"That's not what happened." She needed Wade. She felt so alone with all those men staring at her.

"Hush, honey. Save it for the cops." The elderly woman who had turned away was suddenly at her side. "I called them, too."

Shit.

The doors slid open and two police officers stepped inside. One was a burly looking man and the other a tough female with dark brown hair pulled back in a tight bun. The man stepped forward.

"I'm Officer Jones. This is my partner, Officer Lonzo. We got a call concerning a disturbance here," the officer said.

Brock pointed her way. "My ex-wife assaulted me."

The man who'd called the police nodded. "I saw it. She smashed him on the head and then maced him. It was awful. Guy's just trying to talk to her and she goes off on him."

The female cop turned to the man. "You saw everything? Were you close enough to hear? What was he saying to her?"

Officer Jones had obviously heard all he needed to hear. "All right. Come on, miss. We're going to sort this out downtown."

He had a pair of handcuffs in his hands. Oh, god. He was going to arrest her and Brock would use it against her in their custody hearing. He might get her sent to jail. If she was sent to jail, Ash would be vulnerable. Her gut churned. He would hurt her son. He might kill him and Wade would have no way to legally protect Ash.

No one would listen to her. She could tell her story over and over and it would fall on deaf ears. The world threatened to spin. How could she have gotten comfortable? How could she have forgotten? She was in a haze as she felt the officer move in behind her. She glanced over and Brock was a mess, his eyes red, but there was a smirk on his face. He knew he had her. He was going to get what he wanted.

"Hey, could you hold up a minute?" Officer Lonzo was standing beside the elderly woman, but she looked at her partner. "I get it that your ex is giving you hell, but I think something else is going on here. Are there any security cams?"

The asshole eyewitness shook his head. "Don't need security cameras. I saw the whole thing."

"I doubt that since you weren't there when it started. I was at the end of the aisle. I saw him walk up to her," the elderly lady said, pointing a finger at the witness. "She was perfectly happy until he showed up. She's terrified of him. And he put his hands on her when she tried to walk away. I know how a man breaks a woman's arm. That's what he was going to do. How many times has he hurt you, honey?"

Tears pierced her eyes. No one asked her that. Back home they believed anything Brock told them. Here she'd tried to keep it secret. No stranger had ever stood up for her, had ever offered her solidarity.

"Regina, what are you doing?" Officer Jones asked.

"Stopping you from making a false arrest, partner. I want to see the camera footage. I'm going to need names, too." Officer Regina Lonzo took control, pulling out a notepad and glancing around. "I need the cam footage and I'm going to run you both through our system. Is there anything I should know? Were you two married or simply dating?"

"We were married until he went to jail. That was when I divorced him." The words came out of her mouth dull at first, and then gaining steam.

"He wouldn't allow it before, would he?" her savior asked. "My name is Esther Klein and my husband did the same to me. And you won't find anything improper about me. Not even a speeding ticket. My son is on the force. Call him. He'll tell you I'm of my right mind and my eyesight is quite good. His name is Jimmy Klein. He works under Lieutenant Brighton."

That name seemed to work magic on the male officer. Officer Lonzo merely put a hand on her shoulder. "I believe you, Mrs. Klein. Besides, our friend here didn't get that handprint on her arm from having fun." She looked up at her partner. "You gotta slow down and take in all the evidence. No one gets that kind of wound *after* she's maced an asshole."

Genny glanced down at her arm. Sure enough, there was a red handprint where he'd gripped her so tightly he'd almost broken her arm. Something about seeing that mark on her body turned her cold. She'd been fooling herself.

"Damn," Officer Jones breathed. His eyes went steely and he turned his attention to Brock. "I think we should have a talk, sir."

Officer Lonzo gave her a smile. "He'll be good now. Sorry, my partner is going through a rough divorce. I'm afraid it's made him overeager to believe guys. He'll get over it because it's almost always the asshole guy's fault. You okay?"

Genny nodded her head. "I'm all right. It doesn't hurt."

"That's because you're in shock," she said. "It's going to hurt like a mother later. I'm going to get some pictures. You want to press charges?"

Her first instinct was to say no. It never worked and it only got her in more trouble. It would enrage him further.

"You divorced him, hon. Time to make him understand that was final," Esther Klein said.

"He assaulted me," she said, taking a deep breath. "He told me I had to go with him. I'm afraid he's going to hurt my son. He recently took out a five-million-dollar life insurance policy on him and I think he means to collect."

The officer's eyes went wide. "Oh, we'll see about that."

The doors slid open and Wade was suddenly running in, his boots pounding on the floor. His hair had gone a little wild and he was followed by her boss. Ian Taggart walked in at a more leisurely pace, a drink in his hand.

"I made Big Tag drive me in. Oh, baby, are you okay?" Wade was running his hands over her as though he could sense where she was hurt.

"Made me? I live for this shit. Yo, Regina, what's happening? That's my new admin, you know. Did she brutally murder someone? I could buy that." Big Tag took in the scene with a nod of his head.

"I had no idea she was yours." Officer Lonzo smiled and reached out a hand, shaking Ian's. "If she works for you and she hasn't attempted murder yet, she's a saint. Rycroft, she's good. He got handsy with her and she took care of him. We got a witness and I bet the CCTV footage will make everything clear."

Officer Jones had Brock in handcuffs, pushing him along. "Asshole tried to tell me she started it. His witness admitted that this guy paid him a hundred outside in the parking lot to lie. Big Tag. How's it hanging?"

"Like low-hanging fruit, my man. Don't have kids. They're little animals who don't understand Daddy can't make more of them if they hit him in the balls with their Barbie dream houses," Ian replied. "This

Howard? Because I got a file on him I would like to finish up."

Brock was too busy staring at Wade. His eyes glazed over with hate as he looked at the place where Wade touched her. She moved away, breaking the contact.

"I swear to god if you touch her again, I'll kill you." Wade started toward Brock.

Ian moved in front of him. "He didn't say that, Regina. What he meant to say was something else entirely that didn't put a target on his back in case the fucker actually does get killed. I know. I'm trying to train the puppies properly. Why do you think I came here with him? I forgot my water bottle or I'd squirt him in the face. Does anyone have a newspaper I can roll up?"

Her boss's humor was utterly lost on her. Genny had gone numb again as though it was her only defense. She was cursed and she was going to bring Wade into it. He was already in it. Brock was looking at him like he couldn't wait to wrap his hands around Wade's throat.

She would get him killed.

She'd been stupid, thinking she could have something for herself. She watched as they hauled Brock away, but she knew he would be out in hours if not days. And he would come after them again.

"Baby, talk to me." Wade had turned away and was getting into her space. He pulled her into his arms and she could feel his heart beating. "I thought I would show up too late. I was terrified he would take you."

He would. At some point in time, there would be a reckoning. Brock wouldn't let them be. He would come and if she let it happen, he would take them all down.

"Baby, it's okay." Wade looked back at his boss. "Maybe we should take her to the hospital. I think she's in shock."

Ian didn't say a word, merely stared at her as though trying to figure out what was going on.

Officer Lonzo looked back at her. "I need some information from you and I called the EMTs. We need to document that arm."

Wade looked down at her arm and his face went bright red. Ian had a hand on his shoulder, stopping him from going after Brock.

"Cool down, Wade. You can't kill him in front of the police. Why don't you go and get Genny a bottle of water?" At least Ian was calm. "I'll wait here with her. Take a deep breath and don't make things worse for her."

Wade nodded and walked off toward the deli.

"I'm going to get my tablet so I can make a report. I'll be right back." Officer Lonzo stepped away.

She was left with her boss.

"You're going to do something stupid." Ian sat down on the bench in front of the cash registers.

"You think pressing charges is stupid?" Somehow she hadn't expected that coming from him. Men usually thought the system was fair and that she should try to work within it.

"Nope. I think whatever you're about to do is going to be spectacularly stupid, but I can't stop you. You're going to leave Wade."

He seemed to be a mind reader. "I can't…"

Ian held up a hand. "Yeah, yeah, I get it. You can't put him in danger. He's a trained bodyguard who puts himself in front of bullets for people he doesn't love. It makes no sense for him to do it for the chick he's been pining over for years."

Her boss was excellent at making her feel dumb. "You don't understand."

"I understand better than you think. I'm also smart enough to know that I can't stop you, so I'm going to make you a deal. You let me set everything up. You don't run off on your own."

That wouldn't work. "If I stay here, he knows where I am."

"And if you run, he wins. I'll have Mitch file for a restraining order today. Your custody hearing is in a couple of weeks. We'll let Brock keep his visitation rights."

"What?"

"If we fight him on visitation, we look unsympathetic," Ian said. "Not that I give a shit, but judges take things like that into account."

"But if we allow him supervised visitation, we're trying to work with him," Wade said, holding out a bottle of water. "And we get to pick the supervisors. I think it'll be fun to see how Brock handles it when Ash shows up with Boomer in tow. I hope Brock has a well-stocked fridge."

"Why can't Ash pick if he wants to see his dad?" she said quietly because they weren't done. Not by half. She was putting off the stupid stuff she needed to do.

"If Ash gets on the stand and explains that his dad is abusive, we open it up to questions about why a whole town and legal system neglected to help you," Wade explained. "We can do that, but they'll fight back. We need to get something on Brock, something that will put him back in jail, or strong proof that this is what he's always done and they've been involved in covering it up. We'll get it, but we can't fight this war on more than one side at a time. Get Brock and then we go after everyone who failed you."

His whole world was becoming mired in her problems. Why was he doing this? Guilt. He'd failed her once and he was determined not to do it again. He would give his life to make up for that one mistake.

She'd been wrong to come here. She shouldn't have let Ash talk her into this. "I'm moving out."

Wade's eyes widened. "What?"

Ian took a long sip from his drink. "There it is. I need to make a couple of calls. You two hash this out. Wade, don't have a heart attack."

Well, at least she didn't have to worry about him meddling anymore. She looked up at Wade. "You heard me. I'm moving out."

He frowned down at her. "Over my dead body."

Her hands fisted at her sides. "That can be arranged. I'm leaving and that's it, Wade. I know you don't get this yet, but he could hurt you."

"Let him. I'm ready."

She pointed a finger at him because he was proving her point. "You don't understand how dangerous he is. I do. I'm going to deal with this my way. And it's not the only reason I'm leaving. Moving in with you was stupid. We broke a long time ago and there's no putting us back together. I'm not going to spend one more minute confusing the hell out of my son."

"Don't bring Ash into this. You're not doing this for Ash."

"I'm doing it for me and one day you'll realize I'm doing it for you, too. We jumped into this and we shouldn't have," she explained. "I'm clinging to you because you're familiar. You're trying to save me out of guilt."

He shook his head. "I love you."

"You don't even know who I am."

"How can you say that?"

"Because I don't know who I fucking am, Wade. I have no idea. I was your girlfriend and getting ready to be your wife and then I was his. I've never once been me." Those hated tears were coming now. "When he told me to hang up on you, I did. I didn't even think about it. I obeyed. And when you tell me to do something, I immediately push back. Again, I don't *think*, I react. I've been doing it for so long, I don't know how to do anything else. I can't anymore. I can't be anyone's thing."

He moved in, staring down at her with somber eyes. "I don't see you that way."

"It doesn't matter. I can't see myself as anything else." What did they have if it was so easily crushed? "I want to be on my own. I need to be on my own. Please don't make this hard for me."

His jaw formed a tight line. "I don't understand. How does this help anything? Who's going to protect you?"

"I'm sorry to interrupt, but I need to talk to Ms. Harris." Officer Lonzo was back, her eyes politely on anything but the two of them.

"Don't think this is over," Wade said, stepping back.

But it was. It had to be. She turned to the officer and started to give her statement.

* * * *

It took everything he had not to walk over and pick Genny up and take off for parts unknown. He would stop and get Ash and they wouldn't ever look back.

Except apparently she would. She would look backward and forward until she found a way to get away from him. What had he done? Why was she doing this? It hadn't been five minutes since the cops had shoved Brock in a patrol car and she was thinking of running off on her own?

"You don't have to wait." He could feel Big Tag slide up next to him. The boss had stepped away for a good ten minutes, talking on his phone, probably gossiping like the old biddy his massively muscular body hid inside. Charlotte probably knew what had happened, and soon everyone would know how he'd fucked up.

He just wished he understood. He knew one thing. There was no way he was leaving. "I probably should stay since she's going to need a ride."

Big Tag didn't look at him, simply kept his gaze on Regina and Genny. It had been a stroke of luck that Regina Lonzo had been the officer called to the scene. She worked under Derek Brighton and was also a member at Sanctum. Wade had personally instructed her training group. Regina was smart and did her job with both savvy and compassion.

"I'll take care of her," Big Tag said. "You should stay away from your place for a while. She's going to need a couple of minutes to get her stuff ready."

He turned on his boss. How the hell was this happening? They'd been happy not twenty minutes before. "You're not taking her anywhere. Why the fuck are you helping her?"

"Because someone has to or it's going to go straight to hell. Do you want her out there on her own?" Big Tag nodded toward the door. "Ah, the cavalry is here. Go get a beer and chill, man."

Hutch was walking through the door. He glanced briefly at Genny and then his eyes were on Wade. "Hey, what's going on? Tag told me to get my ass down here."

"I want you to take Wade out. Go grab beers or something. Do that talkie thing so many people do and keep him from killing anyone," Tag said.

"I'm not going anywhere." He couldn't. He had to talk to her, had to make her understand. He sure as fuck wasn't going to waste his time drinking beer.

Tag's eyes narrowed. "She's had a rough day and she's not thinking straight. Don't make this worse on her. I'm taking her somewhere safe, and Jake is already on his way to pick up her son. If you let me, I would like to help her out. She'll stay at Adam, Jake, and Serena's guest house. It's secure and she'll have a panic button if she needs it, but she can be as on her own as she should be right now."

"Genny? She's leaving Wade?" Hutch asked, but there wasn't a terrible amount of surprise in his tone.

Wade turned on the kid. "Don't you even think you have a chance with her. I catch you sniffing around her and you get to see what the inside of your gut looks like, I swear."

He expected Hutch to say something witty, some one-liner that was wholly inappropriate for the situation. Instead, Hutch grew somber. "I flirt with her because it's safe to flirt with her. I wouldn't ask her out because she shouldn't be in a relationship right now."

"What the fuck is that supposed to mean?" The last thing he needed was some kid giving him advice. He had a couple of years and vast amounts of experience compared to Hutch. He didn't spend his life behind a computer screen.

Hutch didn't seem to pick up on his mood. "It means we should grab a beer. There's a bar next door. I'm going. If you would like to know what you're doing wrong with Genny and how you're going to lose her, you can follow me. Or you can push her and then you'll find out on your own."

Hutch turned and walked out.

He looked over at Genny. How could she think what he felt for her was guilt? He was crazy about her. He always had been. Well, except for all those years when he hated her. When he'd left her alone.

"Go with Hutch. I'll take care of her. I'll make sure she doesn't do anything stupid," Big Tag promised.

How could he say that? "You don't think this is stupid?"

Tag finally turned those icy blue eyes on him. "Walking away from you because she needs some space? You thought you could fix her in a few weeks? She's fucked up, man. You can't fix this in bed no matter how much you want to. You can't tell her you love her and magically make her whole again. This is not a problem that's solved with a kiss and a cuddle."

"You don't know a thing about it," Wade spat back, anger curling in his gut.

He shrugged. "Hutch does. Hutch knows a lot about it, but I don't see you running after him in a quest for knowledge."

He couldn't run after anyone. He had to stay close to Genny. His anger deflated in an instant, replaced with a sad inevitability. "I don't want to lose her."

Tag's eyes turned somewhat sympathetic. "Then I suggest you trust your brothers and go get a beer."

"The last time I trusted my brother, she spent fifteen years in hell."

"I'm not your blood, man," Tag said, shaking his head. "And I've learned my lesson. To honor my brothers, I have to take care of the women they love. Even above their own safety and happiness. I learned that a long time ago, so hate me now, but you'll thank me later. Hutch won't wait forever. I don't know how he does it, but he'll be in a broom closet with a waitress before he can finish his first beer, and then he'll be useless."

He glanced back and Genny was still talking to the police. She looked incredibly vulnerable standing there. He felt like if he took his eyes off her for a second, she would disappear. She'd been gone all those years. How could he let her go again? He'd let her down and she'd paid the price and he wasn't going to do it again. She would have to deal with it. He couldn't stand that horrible feeling in his gut. Guilt.

Shit.

Was Big Tag right? Tag damn straight was right about a few things. He had thought he could make love to her and that would somehow magically fix her problems.

Because I don't know who I fucking am, Wade. I have no idea. I was your girlfriend and getting ready to be your wife and then I was his. I've never once been me.

He'd been out in the world, figuring out who he was and what he wanted, and he was still fucked up. What was it like for Genny? She'd only known two men. One had been a boy who'd taken over her life. Yes, he'd done it with love and desire for her, but he could admit he hadn't once thought about changing his life plans to suit her needs. He'd wanted to get out of Broken Bend. He could remember sitting up late nights with his friend Cooper when they traveled the circuit as kids during the summer. Coop had been the one to suggest going into the military. *Hell*, he'd said, *it's gotta be easier than tangling with bulls every night.*

She'd had a full ride to UT Austin and he hadn't once thought about her sacrifice.

And then she'd known Brock, who never gave a second thought to her plans either.

Sure, Brock had abused her, but Wade had marginalized her. In his mind, she'd been his wife and the mother of his kids, the keeper of his house and the woman in his bed. Now that he was older, wiser, he could see that he'd meant to get her pregnant as soon as he could. College had been a waste of time for her in his mind.

He was still thinking that way. He was thinking about marriage and kids and her making a home for them. He wasn't thinking about what she needed.

Jesus, was this how real guilt felt? Had he made her small in his mind when she was everything?

Without a word he turned and walked out. He wanted to go straight to his truck and drive away. He could keep on driving. He didn't have to stop. He would leave everything to her and just drift.

But he didn't. He turned and walked toward the bar. He forced himself to open the door and find Hutch sitting at a big table and yes, he was already flirting with the woman who was taking his order.

Hutch looked up as Wade sat across from him. "Make that two and the onion rings. And thank you." He waited until the waitress walked away and then turned serious. "I watched my father beat the hell out of my mom for years. The truth of the matter is I'm not even sure he didn't kill her. He says he didn't, that she fell down those stairs. He had a good alibi. He was in Afghanistan at the time, but he was scheduled to come home that week and I wonder if she didn't look down those stairs and let herself go. I know technically that means she killed herself, but I blame him. I know that the wrong person can make life so brutal that it's meaningless, that the fight doesn't seem worth it."

His gut clenched. He didn't want that for Genny. "She left you behind?"

Hutch shrugged. "He didn't hit me. I think in her mind I would be okay. In that way, she's nothing like Genny. Genny would fight to the death to stay with her son. In other ways, she very much was. After she died, my father remarried and got himself another punching bag. I watched her, too. I watched her go from young and sunny to cold and unforgiving. She turned herself to stone. I think Genny could go that way if you push her too hard."

Wade's heart actually ached at the thought, but there was more to this situation. "She's in danger."

"And Big Tag will mitigate that as much as he can." Hutch nodded as the waitress came back with the beers. "He'll also convince her to stay at McKay-Taggart. Can I ask you when was the last time you did something for her without any thought to what it would get you? I'm not saying it's bad to try to get into a woman's bed. I do it all the time. Big Tag makes me take way too many STD tests. But that's not the point. When was the last time you thought about what was best for her, even if that wasn't you?"

Never. Never once. He'd loved her and then he'd hated her. The result of both emotions had been oddly the same for her. He'd left her alone. When she hadn't complied with his orders, he'd walked away, heartsick, but away all the same. When he'd found out what had honestly happened, he'd moved her lock, stock, and teenaged son into his house, and in his head he'd been planning marriage and more kids, and soon because he wasn't getting any younger.

He. What he wanted. What he needed.

"She needs time away from me."

Hutch sighed. "I'm sorry, but she does. She needs more than that, and it's going to take a master manipulator to get her the help she needs. Or just a big bastard who won't take no for an answer."

Big Tag. "He's thought about this?"

"We've talked about it," Hutch acknowledged. "She starts at the slightest sound. It was comical at first, until I figured out why she does it. She's getting better about standing up for herself, but she still struggles to do it. Alex yelled the other day. He was pissed at something stupid I'd done and we found her in the closet, hiding. She pretended like she got turned around, but something about Alex's voice set her off. She's trying, but she needs more help, and pretending like she can go from one life to another without help, it's a recipe for disaster. I spent a couple of months under Hope McDonald's tender care and when I came out, it took Kai almost a year to convince me she wasn't coming back for me. Genny spent fifteen years with her abuser, had a kid with him, and he's not dead."

A vision of Brock lying at his feet, blood running all over the place warmed him. "He could be."

"And then her chance at happiness will be gone because you'll likely be in jail," Hutch pointed out. "Revenge is for you, not her, brother."

His gut twisted again. He wanted to do something. "What if she can't ever come back to me? What if our relationship will always remind her of what happened?"

"Do you love her enough to take that chance?"

That was easy. "Yes. She'll be safe?"

"Safe as houses." Hutch frowned. "What does that even mean? I spend too much time with Brits. Or watching *Doctor Who*." Hutch looked up as the door came open, and then he was waving for the waitress. "Miss, as they say in *Jaws*, we're going to need a bigger boat. Just bring one of everything on the appetizer menu."

Wade turned and Shane Landon walked in, followed by Michael Malone, Theo Taggart, Deke Murphy, Bear Bennett, and Boomer. Wade had to smile. Boomer's real name was Brian Ward, but no one called him anything but Boomer.

"One of each?" Theo asked, sliding in next to Hutch. "Boomer will eat one of each all on his own. The rest of us will be left fighting over the scraps."

Theo had spent over a year with Dr. McDonald. Longer than Hutch had and he'd come back. He'd come back to his wife and son because Erin had been patient with him. Because Erin had put him first.

"I could eat," Boomer said.

Deke rolled his eyes. "You can always eat. You are a bottomless pit, my man."

Deke had been held for months by jihadists who tortured him. He'd found his way back because his sisters had been patient, never letting up on giving him their love and trust.

Did he love Genny enough to take the chance?

Fucking Tag *was* a manipulative son of a bitch.

"You okay?" Shane asked, sliding into the seat next to him.

He shook his head because he was done pretending. "Nope, but it looks like I'm going to have to deal with it."

Shane nodded. "Okay. I'm here for you. Anything you need. And Dec is coming back into town in a couple of months. Suzanne is filming a few episodes of her show here in Dallas. He thought we might want to hang out and maybe play some video games. He said he needs guy time. Actually, he said he needs human time, but I ignore some of the weird shit he says now. He reads too many comic books. Hey, has anyone noticed that Big Tag is reading comics now? He tries to hide them, but he's got a full run of something called *Demonica* in his desk. What's up with that? Is he finally going to the dark side?"

It would be good to spend time with Dec and Shane. And maybe he would invite a friend of his own.

He sat and listened to his brothers, joking and talking and basically being brothers. The sorrow was still there, but now hope bloomed inside him, too. His brothers had made it through that fire. And Genny would, too.

While she worked on her problems, he would work. He would find a way to be a better man. All he needed was a little patience.

Chapter Ten

Genny's hand shook as she raised the coffee mug to her lips. It had been two whole days since she'd seen Wade, two days spent settling into another house. Two days spent pretending like she wasn't dying inside.

Had he gone to the club that night and found someone who wasn't damaged beyond all repair? She'd sat up most of that first night envisioning Wade with any number of gorgeous submissives. They could give him what he wanted. She wasn't sure she could.

"Hey, how's it going at the new place?" Charlotte Taggart walked into the break room. She grabbed one of the blue mugs emblazoned with the MT logo and poured herself some coffee.

How was it going? Somber. Sad. Ash had taken one look at her arm and hung his head. He'd picked out his room at the new house without another word. God, she would have felt better if he'd argued with her, cussed at her. Instead he'd been quiet and contemplative. She'd caught him on the phone once and had been sure he was talking to Wade but hadn't asked.

"It's good. The guest house is comfortable. Serena is a gracious hostess." They'd been invited to meals and Jake had escorted her to the grocery store so she could cook for her and Ash. It had been odd to watch the threesome function as a family. Three people who needed each other, who picked up where one left off and never seemed to falter.

"You're safe there. Is one of the guys taking Ash to school and you to work?" Charlotte asked.

"Jake," she replied. "Adam's been busy. He's having some kind of trouble with that computer assistant thing of his."

And speak of the devil. Adam stormed in, his eyes narrowed.

"Charlotte, where's your husband? Did he think I wouldn't figure this out?"

Charlotte put the mug down. "Figure out what? What did he do?"

Adam's jaw tightened and he held up his phone, pointing the camera at his face. "Tess, do a full facial recognition."

Tess's voice came over the phone. She'd gotten used to the sound. Adam used his personal digital assistant for everything. "The input from your peripheral device was not detected. Perhaps you should use a larger device."

Charlotte shrugged. "I don't…"

Tess wasn't finished. "After all, that's what works for Serena."

Charlotte put a hand over her mouth to stifle a laugh. "I will make him fix that."

"It gets worse." He changed the position of his phone slightly. "Try again, Tess."

"Facial recognition complete," the voice said. "One hundred percent match. Welcome back, Douchey McDouche Bag."

Adam shook his head. "Do you know the sad part? I thought about changing her voice to a male voice because I almost found it soothing. It's weird to not be here every day having my ass handed to me by Big Tag."

Charlotte was smiling as she put a hand on his shoulder. "He misses you, too. Teasing you is his way of showing affection."

"He needs to come up with another way," Adam shot back.

Genny took that as her cue to leave. She stepped out and wondered if Wade was in his office on the floor below, or had he taken an assignment? She hated that she didn't know, but she was right to leave.

That moment with Brock had let her know she was frozen and pretending everything was fine. She wasn't ready for a relationship.

She'd let them all down. Wade and Ash. She even thought she'd let down her boss. He'd been kind when he'd driven her back to Wade's and then to Jake and Adam and Serena's place, but she sensed he'd been thinking the whole time. Likely about how to handle her, how to get a new assistant. She wasn't his problem. She had been Wade's and now she wasn't.

She was drifting and taking advantage of people, and that would have to stop at some point.

There was a rose sitting on her desk. She stopped and looked at it.

It sat on top of a book. A couple, actually. Dallas County Community College schedule of classes. There was a sticky note that said *If you want to start small.* And a thicker catalog for UT Dallas. Its sticky note said *But you know you want to be here.*

Wade. Tears made her vision watery.

She sniffled and set her mug down. She couldn't go back to school. It had been too long and she was old now. God, she felt old today. She picked up the rose. It was a sweet gesture. Now that she thought about it, Wade had never been a hearts and flowers guy. He'd never actually given her a present. He'd taken her out and treated her well, but no gifts. They'd been young and poor.

It was the first time anyone had given her flowers.

"Harris, we've got a meeting. Grab your purse and let's go. Quick because I've heard Adam's here and I want to avoid him as long as possible. Tess hasn't even said half the shit Hutch and I programmed her to say." Big Tag was pulling on a jacket as he walked out of his office. "We'll go down the back way. Adam's loafers cost too much for him to ever let them touch a service elevator."

She grabbed her purse and started following Ian, trying not to think about the rose she'd left behind. Ian pushed the button for the elevator. The big industrial doors slid open and they got in. As she turned, she saw Adam at the end of the hall.

"You asshole!" Adam started jogging toward the elevator.

Ian gleefully pushed the *close door* button. "Have fun with the new missus. We programmed her to come on in the middle of sex to grade your performance. I've heard she's a harsh taskmaster, man."

The doors closed before Adam could stop them. She could still hear the *fuck you* reverberating as the elevator moved down.

Ian smiled. "Damn, I miss that asshole."

Sometimes she didn't understand her boss.

He was quiet for the rest of the way to the parking garage, where she climbed into his massive Lincoln Navigator and settled in.

"Where are we going?" It might be good to get out of the office for a while.

"Not far." He pulled out of the garage and into the light of the afternoon. "It's only a couple of blocks, but Adam might follow me, hence the car."

She didn't think so. It didn't matter. She would take whatever notes

Ian needed her to take. She would get through the afternoon. If she got into her job enough, she wouldn't think about Wade and the look on his face when she'd told him she was leaving.

The streets raced by and before she knew it, Ian was pulling into the drive of a lovely building. A valet opened her door, offering her a hand down. Ian slipped the man some cash and his keys before leading her into the building. "Ah, they're right on time. And look, they brought the kid. Thank god. The last time I met with Julian, I had Seth with me and they gave me shit. Not Julian, those two assholes I trained and who have absolutely no respect for me. But Natalie, you look lovely today. Thank you for helping me out."

Ian was talking to a young woman with bright pink hair. She smiled and stood up from the couch where she'd been sitting between two stunningly hot twin brothers. One was dressed in jeans and a T-shirt, the other in slacks and a button-down, but one had an accessory. Slacks man held an infant against his chest, the baby holding her head up off the man's shoulder and looking at the world around her with big, bright eyes. She could tell the baby was a girl because of the pink bow holding back her tuft of hair.

Natalie opened her arms and hugged Ian. "It's good to see you. And you know Ben has the utmost respect for you. I can't do anything about Chase. He respects no one."

"Only you, Cotton Candy," Slacks said.

Ian seemed to remember his manners. "This is my admin, Genny Harris. Harris, these are old friends of mine. This is Nat and her husbands, Ben and Chase Dawson. They're like Adam and Serena and Jake. She married Ben, and Chase came along for the ride."

Slacks rolled his eyes and gently bounced the infant in his arms. "I told you, Tag, I saw her first. She was totally mine. Ben is the candy thief. He only got in because Nat thought he was me."

Nat groaned. "I can't believe we're still arguing about this. Thank god. Kate, we're over here."

She turned and a lovely woman was walking in. She smiled and hugged Nat. She introduced herself to Genny as Kate Roberts-Scott.

"Mason and Cole are already in the gym, Ian. Welcome to the group, Genny. I think you're going to like it. I'll see you inside." Kate walked toward a set of ornate doors. They were opened by a suited bellman, and Genny caught sight of a circle of chairs and women drinking coffee. Before the doors closed again, she could see the other women welcoming Kate.

"We should go in," Nat said, gesturing toward the door.

Genny shook her head. "I'm sorry. I'm here to take notes for Ian."

Ian turned to her. "No, you're here to go through that door. You don't have to talk if you don't want to, but you do have to listen. If you don't want to come back, we won't. If it works for you, if you feel even the slightest bit better, well, I have a standing meeting here every week for the time being and I'll be more than happy to drive you."

She glanced back at the door where Nat was walking through. That was some kind of a therapy session. This was an intervention and with people she didn't even know.

"Or I can call an Uber and leave here now." Who the hell did he think he was?

"You can," he admitted. "But you know you won't ever get better if you continue down the road you're on. I brought you here because *I* got better here. Oh, I'm sure Leo would say I didn't get better until Charlie came back to me, but I didn't murder anyone who didn't deserve to be murdered, and I give Leo Meyer all the credit for that. He doesn't run this group. His ex-wife does, but Janine is one of the best. Leo's current wife is part of the group. New wife getting help from old wife should tell you how good she is."

A group? She didn't have to ask what the group was about. She was sure it was a bunch of sad sacks who couldn't get away from their abusers. He couldn't force her to get freaking therapy.

But then she would lose her job. Maybe she should go in order to keep her job.

She didn't have to talk.

"I don't like that you manipulated me."

Ian shrugged. "It's kind of what I do. If I hadn't manipulated you, we would have had to talk about this. Now we only had to say a few things and then we're cool. What do you have to lose? One session and you can be done and I won't mention it again. Hey, Si. How's it going?"

Simon Weston was one of the employees who'd left with Adam and Jake. He'd visited the house with his wife, Chelsea, the other night. The Brit was wearing a fashionable suit. He stopped and shook hands with Ian.

"As well as can be expected." He held a gym bag in his hand. "I'm going to change. Please tell me we're taking the bastards down today. Why did Chase and Ben bring their kid? I hope they don't think I'll go easy on them because the baby is adorable. My wife is pregnant and mean. I rather need to beat on someone. Genny, it's good to see you here. It's an excellent group. They helped Chelsea enormously."

"I'll catch you on the court," Ian said.

She was quiet until she was sure Simon was out of earshot. "So while I have to join the battered wives' club, you're going to play some basketball?"

"You're just going to rail against the machine, aren't you?" Ian said with a sigh. "I'm going to tell you something almost no one else in the world knows. We play basketball, sometimes we spar. What we also do is talk about how to support our wives. Leo runs the group and he thinks he's good at sports. He's not, but he *is* good at helping people. My and Si's wives were abused by their dad, so I like to think of them as battered daughters, maybe. Ben and Chase and Mason and Cole, Kate's husbands, their wives were kidnapped and held in a cage for months and months of their lives. Leo's wife, Shelley, married a man a lot like Brock. They work hard to survive that every day. If you think they have nothing to teach you about how to take back your life, then you don't have to return. But I'm going to go play basketball and welcome the newest member of our group. Wade, it's good to see you. We have to take down the twins and make sure Si doesn't hurt himself. He's British and double dribbles like a motherfucker."

She looked at the man walking in. Wade Rycroft was simply gorgeous, heartbreakingly beautiful, even with a somber look on his face.

He was going to play basketball and talk to other men whose wives had been through something terrible, men who wanted to love them and support them.

Damn tears were going to be the death of her.

"Genny." Wade tipped his head before handing one of the two bags he was holding to Tag. "I hope you find this helpful. If you don't…"

God, they were trying to do something wonderful for her and she was pushing them away because she could. Because they were safe. Because they wouldn't hit her or spit bile her way, so it was okay to take her anger out on them.

"It'll be good," she said, her voice a bit shaky. She would try it. If Wade was here, she could try, too. Maybe it would help him through his guilt.

And your fear. Your fear that all that's between you is your need and his guilt.

She turned and walked up to the door. The bellman nodded her way and opened it. She walked through and found a seat close to Nat and Kate.

A pretty woman in a stylish suit sat down across from her. "We should get started. For those of you who are new, I'm Dr. Janine Halloway and this is our group. We are survivors, not victims. We are strong enough to face what happened to us, smart enough to want more for ourselves, and brave enough to open our hearts again. That is our goal. That and to love and support each other. Nothing said in group will be talked about outside this room and nothing is off limits. Now, who would like to start today?"

On shaky feet, she stood. "My name is Geneva Harris."

She took a deep breath and began her tale.

* * * *

Thus began the next two months of her life. She worked. She went home and spent time with her son and the Dean-Miles family. Once a week she went to her group and felt terrible as she watched Wade join his. Twice a week, Jake or Adam would drop Asher off with his therapist, Kai Ferguson. Yep, everyone was in therapy and while she was happy the men in her life were getting what they needed, she couldn't help the guilt that welled up inside her.

She talked about that in group, too. Apparently feelings were meant to be felt and acknowledged and worked through. She would inevitably end up crying, her eyes red but her body relaxed as she would come out of the group meeting. Often she would meet up with Wade, who usually showered and changed, though one time he'd stayed in his shorts and muscle shirt, sweat still clinging to his body. His "therapy" involved a lot of working out.

She'd watched him, wondering what he and the others talked about. Was Big Tag encouraging him to let her go or asking him to be patient?

Wade never talked to her unless she approached him. He almost always simply tipped his head in acknowledgement and walked on.

Though that didn't mean he ignored her. Nope. It might be easier if he did.

What was he doing tonight? Evening was coming on and she never looked forward to the weekends. She ended up alone, more or less. Brock was back in Houston and McKay-Taggart was monitoring him in some mysterious McKay-Taggart ways. They had a temporary custody order in place, giving her full custody of her son because of the restraining order. She was safe for now. Ash had something to do almost every night of the weekend. He had friends over or he went out with them. She was also certain he talked to Wade almost every day. Though he didn't mention it, she knew Wade had taken on the duty of picking up Ash from school.

She would read a book or watch some movie everyone in the universe had seen years ago. She would try not to think about Wade.

The truth was this time alone had already been good for her. Something had eased inside her. She was figuring out what she liked and didn't like when no one else came into it.

It didn't hurt that even though he was giving her time, he also found ways to let her know he was thinking of her. He would leave things on her desk, sometimes romantic items like flowers, but also things like movies he thought she would like or magazine articles about career changes. Like she'd had a career to change. He'd left her a thumb drive that said *Play Me*. When she'd put it on, Jason Isbell's "If We Were Vampires" had played, followed by Guns N' Roses's "Patience" and a list of other songs that somehow touched on their relationship.

Damn she loved that man. And she was starting to think they might have a chance.

There was a knock on her door and she started. Damn it. That was one thing she might never get over. The mansion in Broken Bend had always been quiet. Her mother-in-law had insisted on it, and violations would be punished. Brock would slam the door and she would know she was in trouble because he would only do that when his mother was out. Every loud sound made her jump.

She took a deep breath and got up. It was likely Serena inviting her to dinner. She opened the door and her heart rate sped up.

Wade was standing there, looking utterly delicious in jeans and a T-shirt and those scuffed-up boots he loved. She knew what was under those clothes and she wanted more than anything to put her hands on him. That wasn't fair and she wouldn't do it, but she wanted to.

Except he wasn't alone. Shane Landon and Hutch were with him and a man she'd never met, but she'd seen his picture. Declan Burke. He was a tall, attractive man with blond hair and piercing eyes. Apparently Wade didn't know any non-sexy dudes.

"Hi." Why did she have to sound breathy? And why was he here?

He smiled, a slow, sexy expression that went straight to her pink parts.

Yep, she'd needed the time to herself, but she missed him. She still needed the time. Damn it. "Uhm, I wasn't expecting you. I'm sorry. I'm not really ready for company."

His grin turned rueful. "I'm the one who's sorry, darlin'. We're not here for you. Is Ash ready?"

A door in the back slammed and Ash jogged out, dressed a whole lot like Wade. Lately she'd noticed his sloppy-looking sweatpants had been exchanged for jeans and T-shirts he actually tucked in and he'd found a pair of cowboy boots at a thrift store he'd begged her for. Now she realized he was emulating the first man in his life to give him positive attention.

"Hey, guys. I'm ready." He grimaced a little as he looked at her. "Sorry, it was a last-minute invite."

Wade frowned. "No, it wasn't. We've been planning this for a week. Genny, is there a problem? Should I not take him out? We've got tickets to a Marvel movie marathon."

She bit back tears. "Of course he can go." She looked at her son. "Baby, I wouldn't stop you from going out with him. I know you're friends and I'm grateful for that. You don't have to hide it or spring it on me at the last minute. I'm good."

Ash breathed an obvious sigh of relief. "Thanks, Mom. You should probably know that we're going to the rodeo next week and Wade's going to start teaching me self-defense again."

God, he was incredibly good to her and Ash. "I think that's wonderful."

"All right then," Wade said gruffly. "Go on to the big house, Ash. Jake's going with us, too. Adam said he's got some emergency. Apparently that robot assistant of his recently ordered a stripper for him. A male stripper. He showed up at the office as a police officer and then proceeded to strip in the middle of a staff meeting."

Hutch snorted. "Yeah, I heard there was a lap dance involved."

She knew a guilty man when she saw one. "You and Ian have to stop that."

Hutch grinned, the smile making him look young and carefree. "I have no idea what you're talking about. Come on, Ash. I have candy for us to smuggle in."

"Awesome. Later, Mom." Ash kissed her on the cheek and ran off behind Hutch.

"I'll go get Jake," Shane said.

Declan held his hand out. "I'm Declan Burke. I've heard a lot about you, Genny. And I have a gift from my wife. These are her homemade chocolate chip cookies. She's an amazing cook. I was told if I ate them instead of giving them to you, she would do terrible things to me. Given who her father is, here are the cookies all intact. She wanted me to tell you that everything works out when you're brave enough."

Okay, that was weird, but she liked cookies. She took the bag. "Thank you and please tell her I'm grateful."

He nodded as he followed Shane.

Wade lingered. "Dec thinks his father-in-law is some kind of demon. I would worry about him, but I'm pretty sure that's how a future son-in-law is going to describe Big Tag one day. Are you doing okay? Don't think because I'm giving you space that I'm not thinking about you pretty much every second of the day. But I understand we moved too fast."

They had. She got that too, but she was starting to think they could try again. "We can't pretend nothing happened and pick back up where we left off."

"I know that now. I don't even want to. That wasn't good for you. We need to get to know each other the way we are now." He held a hand out. "My name is Wade Rycroft and I think you might be the prettiest girl I've ever seen. If you don't mind me saying so, ma'am."

There were the tears again. She put her hand in his, his warmth tempting her. "Geneva Harris. And I don't mind. I'm a single mom. We like to hear we're pretty."

"I like your son very much," he said. "I was wondering if you would like to go to the rodeo with us. It would be a no-pressure date. I promise to behave like a gentleman. I also promise not to indulge your son in as much sugar and soda as he's going to have tonight because it's boys' night and we go crazy on the candy and soda. There might be popcorn involved. Though if you come with us to the rodeo, I can promise you a corn dog."

A date, but a safe one. No pressure, just two old friends getting to know each other again and introducing her son to something that should have been his birthright. "I think I would like that."

He tipped his hat her way. "Then I will pick you both up at six next Saturday. And I'll have Ash home before midnight."

Ash would be utterly safe with this man. "Thank you for being good to him."

"I love that kid. You have a good night, Genny." With a smile, he turned and walked off.

Genny closed the door behind her. What to do since she had a whole night to herself?

The catalog of classes Wade had left on her desk caught her eye.

She picked it up. It couldn't hurt to look through it.

She sat down and for the first time started thinking about her future.

Chapter Eleven

Wade pivoted and took a hard elbow from one of the twins. When they weren't talking, it was hard to tell them apart. When they were talking it was easy.

"Shoot, old man. You afraid to shoot? Do the eyes not work so great anymore?"

That was Chase Dawson. Wade absolutely could believe Ian had trained that man. That asshole had several years on him, but he was the old man? "I'm not afraid to shoot you."

He took his shot, delivering the ball straight into the basket.

Chase picked up the ball and tossed it to his brother, Ben. "Yeah, well, there are days when I stand in front of the windows I told Nat we shouldn't put in the house because we're going to get sniped and I beg for someone to come and take me."

Ben paused, dribbling in place in front of Simon, who really couldn't play basketball. "Greer is teething. Chase can't stand it when she cries. You know this is going to be you in a couple of months, Weston. And you can't even split the duties. No sleep for you."

"I'm not getting any bloody sleep right now." Si leapt up and batted down the pass. "It's like Chelsea turns on around ten o'clock. She's tired all day and then when she should sleep, she's manic. The good thing is once she's done with all the morning sickness—and morning is a misnomer—she's horny. I've had more sex since she got pregnant than I did when we were trying to get pregnant. I can't believe I'm saying this, but I think my wife is using me like a living vibrator."

Okay, the Brit was getting better. All this talk about kids was slightly upsetting. What if Genny didn't want more kids?

Ben grinned as Leo handed him the ball and he tossed it back into play. "Enjoy it now, my man. Take all that sweet loving you can get because it stops when the baby's born."

They went on, Ian talking about how Charlie was trying to get his sperm again because she wanted one more small demon to round out the group. Chase swore they'd had their last, but Ben shook his head as though that decision had already been made.

They all had kids. Or were in the process of having them. Leo's wife, Shelley, had recently given birth to their first, a baby boy.

He forced himself to move, years of physical exertion making the motions habitual. His brain was racing though. Could he be okay not having the whole baby experience? It was odd because he'd never thought about it before, would have told anyone who asked that he didn't care. It was different now that the woman he was thinking about sharing a life with was Genny.

"You okay, Wade?" Leo was backing Big Tag toward the sidelines. It was three on three today.

"I'm good." He said it out of habit. This was not the place for habit. This was the place where he was supposed to be honest about what he was feeling. The trouble was he wasn't used to admitting he felt anything at all. Still, maybe talking about it would help, and all these guys were dads or almost dads. "I was wondering if Genny's going to want more kids. She's got a teen. Why would she start again?"

"You can have one of mine," Big Tag offered helpfully. "Kala is a sweetheart. She's loving and kind. Everyone should have such a daughter."

Chase stopped in the middle of the court, his jaw open. "She's the devil. When we had play group at our house, she tried to teach Chloe Lodge how to build a fire."

Tag shrugged. "She might need that skill one of these days."

"In the middle of my office? She used my reports as kindling," Chase shot back.

Leo called a time-out. "Guys, I don't think this is helpful. Wade's asking an honest question. Obviously we don't know what's going through Genny's head, but this is something you need to think about."

Tag grabbed a bottle of water. "Genny's not exactly old. She started young. She's at the age when a lot of women are starting families. She's younger than Charlie, and I can't get that woman to stop spitting out kids. Grace did it. I think you should talk to her."

"And I think you should consider carefully how you discuss this with her," Leo said.

Her words from the grocery store came back, haunting him every day.

I can't be anyone's thing.

She'd been her father's daughter, his girlfriend, Brock's trophy wife, Ash's mom. When had Geneva Harris ever simply been herself? "Is it even fair of me to ask?"

Ben wiped sweat off his brow. "You can't think that way. You're a part of this relationship, too. Well, you would be if you *had* a relationship with her."

He shot Ben the finger. "We have a relationship. We're dating."

It was nice. The drama had ratcheted down significantly. They'd fallen into a pleasant routine. He took her to lunch once a week, giving her the space to find her place at work. She'd found a group of female friends. She spent time with Shane's wife, Talia, and had gotten quite close to Nat and Kate from her group. On Friday nights, he took her to dinner and then they met Ash, picking him up from whatever he was doing with his friends that night. On Saturdays they went out, all three of them, or stayed in and ordered pizza. They would play games or watch movies.

No sex. He'd kissed her last Saturday night, a brief brushing of lips that hadn't even begun to satisfy him. He wanted more. He wanted to stay with them.

"I think what Ben is trying to say is that it's easy for us to forget that we're part of this, too. When your significant other has gone through the kind of trauma yours has, it's natural to suppress your own needs," Leo said, sounding like the academic he was. "It's also a mistake. You have to sit down and talk to her. Before you do that, though, you have to know what you can accept and what you can't. If she's horrified at the thought, how are you going to handle that? Do you want a relationship with her if she doesn't want kids?"

That was an easy answer. "Yes. I want her more than I want anything."

"Good, then you can open a dialogue when she's ready to talk about the future," Leo said.

"And what if she's never ready?" That was his real fear. He knew they were getting back to a point where sex would be on the table. But he wasn't sure she would want to marry him, want to build a home with him.

"Patience," Big Tag said, putting a hand on his arm. "She'll get there. She's already more comfortable at work. She regularly puts me on my ass. I think she's taking lessons from Charlie. And if you need to take out your aggression, punch Chase in the face. He deserves it."

Chase flipped him off, but then from what Wade could tell that was half of the man's communication skills.

"Ian is an ass, but he's also right," Leo said. "She's coming along nicely and you're a huge part of that. By being patient and letting her know she can take the time she needs and not lose you, you've given her a gift. She's learning that she's safe with you, and she's also getting the time to figure out you're not here because you feel guilty."

The door to the small gym flew open and Shane ran in, his face flushed. "Wade, man, you aren't answering your cell."

He left his cell in the locker room when he was on the court. Leo didn't allow cell phones during his "sessions." A wave of fear went through him. Shane had come all the way over from the McKay-Taggart building. He wouldn't have done that if things weren't serious. As they were only working on training right now, there was exactly one thing that would put that look on Shane's face. "We lost him?"

Shane nodded. "The PI we were paying down in Houston said he hadn't come out of his apartment for over forty-eight hours. He's gone. We have no idea where Brock Howard is. I'm sorry, Wade."

Ian grabbed his shirt, dragging it over his head. "No, this is my fault. I haven't wanted to hire anyone and that's why we're working with contractors. Shane, did we send someone to pick up Ash?"

"Jake's on his way to the school. We need to secure Genny." Shane frowned as he reached into his pocket, pulling out his cell. "Shit. He's calling someone."

"We managed to dupe his phone?" Big Tag asked.

"The contractor wasn't a bad PI." Wade was already in motion. He had to get to Genny. Luckily she was here at Lodge's building. She was having lunch with Kate and Nat after group, so she should be safe for the moment. "But you know as well as I do that 24/7 coverage is hard to maintain. He tagged Brock's phone early on, but Brock also has a landline. We haven't caught him doing anything but ordering pizza and talking to his lawyer."

Shane turned the phone around. "He's not talking to the lawyer today. That's Genny's number. I'm going to listen in."

"Give it to me," Wade said. Had Brock been calling anyone but her, he would have put it on speaker.

She knew he'd had Brock's phone tagged, but he wasn't sure she would remember. Maybe she wouldn't pick up. She might hate him for it later, but he wasn't leaving her alone. Not ever again.

"Hello, wife."

Wade listened to the conversation, to the way Genny's voice hitched when she realized who she was talking to, to the horror and sorrow in her tone. His stomach turned. Brock had done it. He'd managed to do the one thing sure to make Genny lose her mind and her good sense.

She was going to leave him. She was going to sacrifice herself. And he would have to stop her. He would have to take control when he'd promised her he wouldn't.

She would never forgive him this time.

* * * *

Her cell phone trilled and she thought about ignoring it. It was a lovely afternoon and the sun was shining through the windows, making the small dining room feel warm and cozy. Everyone called this place The Club. She'd learned it was an alternative to Sanctum run by one of Ian's first investors, a man named Julian Lodge. He was the one who had set up the sessions and offered his building as the meeting place. He also had this small private dining room for friends and club members, of which Nat and Kate were both.

"Oh, you're going to love Top," Nat was saying. "The food is heavenly. It's such a surprise to me that almost all the chefs are straight out of the military. If I'd had to guess I would have said they'd all spent their lives cooking in some ridiculous French culinary school."

Kate laughed, the sound musical. She was a lovely woman with rich brown and gold hair. The fact that she could smile at all after what she'd been through seemed like a miracle to Genny. If Kate had gotten through and managed to find a life, she could, too. "I think after having to eat all those MREs, military men and women are focused on eating well."

She was supposed to go to this restaurant everyone seemed to love next Friday night. It was a hot spot run by Ian's brother Sean Taggart. She and Wade had been keeping things fairly casual, but he'd told her Top was more classy than the beer and burger joints they'd been going to. She'd picked them because they felt comfortable and not at all date-like. She got the feeling this was Wade's way of pushing her a little.

Of course, after weeks and weeks of not sleeping with him, maybe she was ready to be pushed a little. The kiss he'd given her last Saturday night had made her wish she'd invested in a vibrator.

No, it hadn't. It made her wish she could trust the bond between them, that she didn't have to lose herself in a relationship with him.

Hours and hours of talking, getting to know him again, had made her certain he was the right man for her. He was loyal to his friends, always tried to do what was right, would be the best father in the world.

She wanted more kids. It was something she'd confronted in group, the idea of starting over. She loved her son, but she wanted to start a family the right way, with love and not fear in her heart. She wanted to be excited about the pregnancy, to have her husband sitting beside her holding her hand this time and know that he'd be good to their child. She wanted a partner and to safely know that siblings wouldn't mean more risk, but simply more love.

And that husband wasn't some nameless, faceless somebody. It was Wade Rycroft. It always had been. She wasn't sure how it would have worked out if things had gone their way all those years before. Maybe they would have broken up. Maybe she would have become his deeply submissive wife. Maybe they would have grown together.

What she had learned was that she couldn't look back. She could only move forward, and she was ready to start moving forward with Wade.

"You have to get the linguine," Nat said. "The last time we were there, I got the linguine with this ridiculously good lemon sauce. Ben got steak *frites* and loved it. Chase won't go because of the windows. The whole front of the restaurant is this gorgeous bank of windows that overlook the street. Chase is completely paranoid about snipers. I swear sometimes I hope someone will actually snipe him. But then I remember how much I love him."

Her purse was still vibrating. She pulled her phone out. She didn't know the caller, but it could be Ash's school. "Give me a sec. I've got to take this. Hello?"

"Hello, wife."

The whole place seemed to go cold. Brock. That was Brock's voice. Nausea hit her. She'd hoped she wouldn't have to hear from him again except through their lawyers. "You're not supposed to contact me."

A nasty chuckle came over the line. "No, I'm not allowed to come within five hundred feet of you, my love. I can call you all I like. After all, we share a child and we have to decide on his welfare together." His voice sent a shiver down her spine.

"You don't care about Ash." What a joke.

"Call him by his name. You know I hate the fact that you use his middle name. Ash isn't a name. It's something that happens when you burn a house down. He's Brock Howard the fourth, and no matter how many idiot cowboys you throw at him, they'll never be his father. Now I want to talk to you. In person."

She stood up, moving away from the table, but she could see Nat was already concerned. "I won't meet with you. I'm not insane and I'm done being your punching bag. Don't try to come near me because Wade will enforce that restraining order. I promise you that. Contact my lawyer."

"I've had a talk with that pit bull Rycroft hired for you. He's not a pleasant man. And it won't work. I don't recognize the divorce. We were married in front of God and you can't change that."

Well, she'd expected that argument. "By the laws of this country, I damn sure can. You signed those papers, Brock. We're divorced."

His voice went low, betraying his anger. "I signed them because my lawyer said fighting you while I was trying to negotiate the best plea bargain I could get was a bad idea. I have you to thank for that, too. We'll discuss that later, my love. And you need to understand you'll pay for fucking that piece of shit cowboy. I won you a long time ago."

"Won? You blackmailed me and then you continued to do it with my son. Like I said, if you want to talk to me, call Mitch. He can speak for me." She was ready to hang up and then she would find Wade and tell him Brock was fucking around with her again. He was her bodyguard, or at least the bodyguard in charge of her case. She had a file in Big Tag's system and everything.

"I have our son."

The room went downright arctic. "What?"

He let that sit for a minute and when he spoke again, he sounded lighter, happier. As if he knew he was in control now. "I know you had a good plan. Junior was perfectly safe in that school. You and the big thug drop him off and some other thug comes and picks him up, but our little boy is naughty. I think he's had some bad influences in his life lately. He cut class with some friends of his. They were going to pick up a video game or something, and that's when I decided to spend some father/son time with him."

"I don't believe you." It couldn't be true. Ash was safe in his school. Ash wouldn't have done something like that. Except lately he'd been rebelling. Not against her exactly, but his life had been so regimented that he'd gone a bit crazy with his new freedom.

"All right. I can see I have to prove it to you. You know everything you've done lately simply makes me believe you need discipline. I'll punish you for not believing me. You'll remember that when I say something is true, you don't question me. For now, here's your proof. Son, Mommy doesn't think you're here."

"Don't give him anything, Mom. Get Wade." Her baby boy sounded like he'd been screaming. His voice was mottled.

Her heart clenched and her vision threatened to fade, but she wasn't about to pass out. She couldn't. "What are you doing to him?"

"Nothing much. The boy needs discipline, too. I think that's where I went wrong with him. I ignored him. I did that for you, you know. My love for you blinds me sometimes. I'll do more if you don't come here right away. And if you tell that boyfriend of yours anything, I'll kill Junior. You're to come alone and then the three of us will leave the country. I'm only trying to keep my family together. It's what a good father does."

She was getting weak in the knees. "Where do I go?"

"First off, you'll meet me someplace public, but you need to understand that I've hired some people. I'll have one of them stay here with our son. If I get even a hint that you haven't come alone, I'll send the guard the signal to kill him. If I don't make contact with him in a timely manner, our son will be killed."

"And you call yourself his father."

"I'm the head of this family and you and our son are mine to do with as I wish. You both belong to me and if I decide to take you out, I will. You should remember that. You will come back to me and play your part."

Play her part. Wade might have once seen her as his potential wife, but that wasn't a part for her to play. She forgave herself in that moment. They'd been children. She'd made a choice and the truth was she would have made it again and again because it brought her Ash. She couldn't have known what would happen then. She only knew what had to happen now. "Yes, Brock. I will. Where do you want me to meet you?"

"I'll text you the address." He was silent for a moment. "I'm very disappointed in you, Geneva. I thought you were better than this. You were always the woman for me. Even when you were a girl. You were the only one who ever saw me."

She'd been too optimistic about him. And she forgave herself for that, as well. It was time to move past the pain and find some damn joy in her life. It was odd that the truth came to her in the midst of her terror.

She'd been here before. She knew what she had to do.

The phone clicked off.

"Genny, are you okay?" Nat asked.

"I have to go." She had to get out of here. With watery eyes, she looked around the small dining room. There was no time. Brock would text her the address and she had to be there when he said. There was no way around that. She had to move quickly if this was going to work.

"I think you should wait here," Kate replied, concern in her eyes. "Nat's already called her husbands."

"You did what?" Why would she have done that?

She didn't get the chance to ask again because the doors opened and she breathed a huge sigh of relief because she didn't have to run through The Club screaming for Wade like a mad woman. He was here.

He would always be here. She knew that now. It didn't matter who they'd been. All that mattered was who they were now.

"Baby, I know what you're going to say…" Wade started.

She barely registered the words. "Brock has Ash. You have to get our boy back. You have to get him back, Wade. He has our boy."

She practically fell into his arms. She didn't have to be strong. She'd saved herself once. This time was all about him. He was the security expert and more than that, he was her man. This was their problem.

She wasn't making the same mistake twice.

Wade's arms went around her and she could feel his sigh of relief. "Baby, I thought you would run off on your own. I thought you would try to sacrifice yourself."

She was confused, but she wasn't about to let go of him. "Who told you? Oh, god, I forgot you duped his phone. You heard it. No, I wasn't going off on my own. Not again. We're in this together. Wade, you have to get him back. He's going to hurt Ash. I think he already has. He's going to kill him and collect that money."

Blood money.

"Where are you supposed to meet him?" Ian was behind Wade. He and Simon Weston stood there with Nat's husbands, Ben and Chase Dawson, and the therapist she'd met, Leo Meyer. Simon was on his phone and Ben and Chase had Nat in between them.

"Adam, I need you to start a citywide search for Geneva's ex-husband," the Brit said. "He has her son. Check the cameras around the school."

"No need," Ian said. "Though please ask Adam to get any camera footage he can of Asher. If we can find footage of that asshole kidnapping him, it'll help enormously when we put him back in prison."

She wasn't sure what Ian was thinking. "I need to know where he's holding my son. Wade, tell him to find Ash."

Wade turned the slightest shade of pink. "I know where Ash is. I've already got a team on the way. They'll wait for my command. We have to wait until Brock shows to the meeting with you, baby. I promise you, they'll take care of Ash."

"My brothers, Theo and Case, are on their way along with Michael and Bear. They'll surround the apartment where he's holding Ash and take down his little friend when we give the signal," Ian explained.

"How do you know?" She didn't really care. He'd done exactly what he'd said he would. He'd protected them. She didn't care that he'd listened in. It merely saved her a couple of minutes of talking.

"I might have put a GPS locator in his backpack," Wade admitted with a wince. "And on his phone. And in his boots. The backpack and phone were left behind in a park. I'm pretty sure Ash is still wearing those boots though."

He was brilliant. "I love you."

He pulled her close. "I love you, too."

Kate smiled, perfectly calm, as though she was certain everything would be all right. "That's much smarter than swallowing it. I lost a good necklace that way."

Nat laughed but reached for Genny's hand. "It's going to be okay."

She took a deep breath and let her man do his job. She'd already done hers.

"I don't want you to do this."

Genny looked over at Wade thirty minutes later. They were in the back of Ian's Navigator, waiting for the go. She was supposed to meet him in a park outside of SMU. The good news was he'd told her to take an Uber and not bring a car of her own. Her "Uber" driver this afternoon would be Alex McKay.

"It's going to be okay." She was calm. She was surrounded by competent people. This was what they did.

She was grateful Wade had found his place with them.

"Alex is here. Boomer is in place. DPD knows he's here." Ian was coordinating from his phone. She'd been shocked at how fast they could move when they wanted to. "Boomer is our sniper. He's going to take Brock out if everything else goes to hell. Otherwise, we'll try to do this by the book."

"Or Boomer could take the shot the minute he has one," Wade argued.

"Do you want Boomer to go to jail?" Ian asked as though he was asking about the weather. "Because I like my taxes low. Boomer hits the penal system and then they have to feed him. Taxes go up and I get irritable."

"It's fine," she said. "I'll be okay. My main concern is that Brock doesn't get the chance to send out that signal. You have to make sure."

"It's already set up," Wade replied. "I wish I could be there. Theo and the boys were closer. He's in South Dallas. I would be stuck in traffic. I hate sitting here."

"Well, that's what you're going to do," Ian replied. "Unfortunately, that bastard was smart to make this public or I'd let you murder him and then we could get rid of the body. Instead we have to deal with a whole bunch of co-eds, and that means we have to outsmart him. Which you already did, Wade. If you need some closure, you can have it in a couple of minutes."

"I have to face him in a couple of minutes," she said. She took a deep breath, telling herself it would be fine.

Adam Miles's voice came over the line in the car. "I've got him. One hundred percent recognition. Tess confirmed it. Of course she also told me I should work out more, but you've got your go."

Wade touched a button on his phone. "Theo, Case, you have a go. Let me know when it's done."

Fear went through her. "You can't do that. We don't have him yet."

Ian winked her way and pointed. "Yeah, we do. That's Lieutenant Brighton and his team. We recorded the conversation between you and dear old Brock. And I think Ash will have something to say, too. Officer Lonzo is working that scene with our guys. She'll gather enough to send this guy to jail forever. Ah, look. Howard just figured out Boomer has a bead on him."

Sure enough, Brock was looking down at the red dot on his chest, his eyes widening.

Wade reached for her hand. "I was never going to let him get near you. Baby, I know you want revenge, but…"

He needed to stop thinking he knew what she was going to do. She leaned over and kissed him for all she was worth, wrapping her arms around him. "Thank you."

He shook his head. "I can't lose you again."

"Never." She smiled up at him, but she still had a few questions. "If I wasn't going to go and meet him, why did Ian call Alex to pretend to be my driver?"

There was a knock on the window and Alex stood there frowning, a bag in his hand. "Your lunch, asshole."

Ian rolled the window down and took the bag. "Thanks. I was hungry. I have to eat this fast or Boomer'll show up. He has the sense of smell of a hungry Rottweiler. Thanks, buddy."

Alex shook his head and then he was grinning. "Hey, your ex peed himself. I thought Brighton had gotten soft. It's good to know he can still handle himself in the field."

She glanced out the window and the police were snapping cuffs on Brock, who was arguing with them.

That was when the Taser came out.

Wade's phone rang. "Yes? Ash, are you okay? I know. I know, son.

I'm sorry I couldn't be there. Me, too. Here, talk to your mom. She needs to hear your voice."

She forgot all about Brock as she took the phone. "Baby?"

"I'm okay," Ash said, his voice still shaky. "I have seen a lot of things I wish I hadn't, but I'm good. And I'll never complain about invasion of privacy again. I want a tracker implanted in my damn butt. I'm sorry I cussed."

This was one situation she wouldn't complain about. "When you're kidnapped by a madman, you cuss away, baby. You can even say the *F* word."

She sat back, Wade's arms around her as Ash began to tell his tale. They were all safe and Brock would be gone for a long time.

It was a good day.

Epilogue

One year later
Broken Bend

Wade looked out over the reception area, a deep sense of satisfaction in his system. He felt someone move in and knew exactly who it was. His son. He put an arm around Ash. "You did good, best man."

He had a lot of friends and brothers, but only one son for now. In the year since he'd asked Genny to marry him, a lot had changed, including Ash's last name. Asher Rycroft had been adopted formally the night before.

His boy. If they never had another kid, he would be okay, but Genny seemed a bit baby crazy. Between Chelsea Weston's baby girl and Charlotte Taggart announcing her latest pregnancy, Genny had started talking about it.

He just hoped a new baby would help Big Tag get through the dark cloud he was under. Wade feared after what happened in Munich that it would take something more violent to put Tag back on the right track.

That was what pure and utter betrayal could do to a man.

"It wasn't hard. I only had to keep track of the ring. Even if I got lost, I know someone's going to find me." Ash pulled up his tuxedo pants. "I'm wearing these boots until the end of time."

The first night after he'd been rescued had been hard. They'd all ended up sleeping in the same big bed, him wrapped around Genny and her around her son.

Ash kept seeing Kai Ferguson, Wade kept up with his weekly basketball game that was really therapy, and Genny went to her group.

Slowly they'd healed.

The fact that Brock had been found dead in his prison cell hadn't hurt. Wade still wasn't sure Big Tag hadn't arranged that, but he wasn't about to ask. It was done and he wouldn't come back.

"I still appreciated it, son." He liked saying that word. A slow song came on and a pretty girl strode up. Wade didn't recognize her but there was so much family around he wasn't surprised. His family, their work and club family.

"Would you like some punch? The kids are all hanging out together," she said with a shy smile on her face. "I mean the older kids. The younger ones are out on the playground. I'm trying to avoid that. They're kind of crazy."

Ash opened his mouth, but no sound came out.

It was good to know his son still had a couple of things to learn. He was staring at the poor girl like she was the first he'd ever seen. And he liked what he saw.

Wade put a hand on his shoulder. "He'd love to."

"I would," Ash said, finally finding his voice. He trailed off after her.

"I remember being a dumb kid," a familiar voice said. His brother.

"Not yet, Clint." He didn't look at his oldest brother. He'd agreed to have the wedding on the ranch because it had been Genny's dream, a nod to their past, and he thought she hoped for some forgiveness for his brother.

"But someday?" There was no way to miss the sorrow in his brother's voice.

"Maybe." He couldn't give him what he wanted, but he was softening. Clint and Lori had gone all out for this wedding. "I do thank you for the beautiful ceremony."

"Geneva's a beautiful human being. She deserved a beautiful wedding," Clint said. "Lori's pregnant."

"Congratulations. I think there's something in the water. We've got a lot of pregnant women here today." He glanced over where Theo Taggart was gently cupping his wife Erin's growing belly.

Damn but that reminded him that nothing was certain. There were no guarantees. They had to hold on to love with everything they had.

"If it's a girl we would like your permission to name her Geneva," Clint said. "Because we wouldn't be here without her. She saved us all. I know you're still angry…please think about it."

He looked out where his wife was still in her wedding gown, her eyes glowing as she laughed at something Nat said. She would never name a child after herself, but it would be good to have another Genny in his life. His niece. They were standing on the land Genny had saved. "I think that's a great idea."

"Thank you. I'm going to go and see if the car's on its way. We'll make sure Ash has a good time while he's staying out here," Clint promised.

Ash wanted to hang out at the ranch while they were on their honeymoon. Loa Mali was calling their name. A full two weeks on the beach with his gorgeous wife was made easier by knowing Ash would be taken care of. Clint had promised to show him another side of the town he'd grown up in. "I appreciate it. We'll be okay one day, brother."

"I pray for that day." Clint nodded and walked off.

He smiled as he heard the band starting to warm up. Emily and Coop had come. Damn but he'd missed them. Sometimes he was almost certain fate had brought them back into his life. She'd needed a bodyguard and his old friend, Coop, had called him in. Emily had been on the verge of country music stardom at the time, but all Cooper had wanted was the girl he was in love with to be safe. Watching their love story play out had made him ready for his own. He waved at them but made his way to the table he truly belonged at. His groomsmen were sitting together at one table. Once they'd been a team of bodyguards and one by one they'd all fallen—not in the line of duty but into some woman's arms, and that was the best way to fall.

Remy Guidry looked up, a smile on his face. "Hey, there's the man of the hour. I see your old friend is here. Not many people get to say Emily Young was their wedding singer."

Wade was fairly certain that Cajun accent had gotten ten times deeper since Remy and Lisa had moved back to Louisiana to take over his family's business.

He grinned because he was pretty sure everyone was star struck by Emily. "Ah, you know I'm sure she does that for all her friends. She told me she misses playing small venues now that she does her own stadium tours. I say, hey, Em, gotta barn for you right here." He chuckled. "I'm happy she and Coop could make it. Did you get to see Sadie and Chase?"

He missed Sean's spitfire niece, and he liked the hell out of her new husband.

"Yeah, she looks great," Shane said. "I did not tell her that we've gone through three receptionists in the year and a half since she left. No one can handle the big guy's bad temper."

"He does not handle transition well," Declan said.

"He doesn't handle transition at all." Wade had been dealing with the problem for a year and a half. Genny made a million excuses for the boss she'd come to love. "Shane and I have been trying to get him to refill the spots you guys left open. He always finds something wrong with the candidate. Sometimes the candidate walks out in the middle of the interview. One of them actually ran. It's crazy."

"The big guy will come around," Remy said, though his expression told a different story.

"Do you think so?" Riley asked. "After what happened with Ezra and his group? I don't know. He hasn't been the same since."

Munich. It all came back to the Munich op. He hadn't been on it, but he'd been around for the fallout. It was a miracle any of them survived. The men they'd called the Lost Boys had always had the deck stacked against them. They hadn't known the true threat would come from within.

Remy shook his head. "He can't blame himself. No one saw that coming."

"I've told him that same thing a hundred times," Wade replied with a shake of his head. "He's taking the weight of the world on his shoulders."

"No one could have known. He played everyone. We all thought he was…" Shane pushed back from the table. "I don't want to think about him. I want to forget what happened to those men and focus on the fact that we're all good. Our team. We were lucky. We're all whole and here."

It was his wedding night. There would be more than enough time to deal with the way the world had changed since Munich. He was going to take this time to be happy.

Dec slapped Shane on the shoulder. "You're right. Tonight we celebrate."

"The dancing is about to start so grab your girls," Wade offered with a smile.

Remy stood, walking off toward the front of the barn. Wade

thought he was going to look for the boss. He was grateful someone was going to try to pull Ian back into the group.

"Hey, y'all," Emily said, her sweet voice coming over the speaker. "We want to welcome everyone to Broken Bend, Texas, and to the wedding of some special friends of mine. Would Mr. and Mrs. Rycroft like to share their first dance?"

He looked over and Genny was glancing around, searching for him.

He moved to her, his eyes never leaving that face he loved.

He took her hand. They'd kissed for the first time not a hundred yards from here. He'd touched her the first time right here in this barn, his young soul wanting to mesh with hers. Even then he'd known how much he loved her.

"Will you dance with me, Geneva?"

The smile she gave him was past brilliant. "I would love to."

He took her hand as the slow country music filled the barn, the lights above them twinkling like stars.

She was in his arms and he was finally home.

* * * *

Also from 1001 Dark Nights and Lexi Blake, discover Arranged, Dungeon Games, Adored, and Devoted.

Author's Note

When I started this book I wasn't really thinking about domestic abuse. It was a plot line, a way to get these two characters together, but somewhere in the middle of the book, my characters taught me something. Genny had a reaction I didn't think she would have and I realized this subject was far more than a plot device. There are Gennys out there and I pray they all find their Wades, but my hope with this book is to shine a small light on the women and men living in abusive relationships. There is help and hope. And know that your whole book community stands with you.

If you are in an abusive relationship, please contact the National Domestic Abuse Hotline at www.thehotline.org. If you are worried that your computer is being monitored, please find a safe way to call 1-800-799-SAFE. If you are deaf or hard of hearing, call 1-855-812-1011.

Even in the darkest night, the stars are there. Clouds might hide them, but they are there, giving us the hope of light.

Much love,

Lexi

Sign up for the 1001 Dark Nights Newsletter
and be entered to win a Tiffany Key necklace.

There's a contest every month!

Go to www.1001DarkNights.com to subscribe.

As a bonus, all subscribers will receive a free copy of
Discovery Bundle Three
Featuring stories by
Sidney Bristol, Darcy Burke, T. Gephart
Stacey Kennedy, Adriana Locke
JB Salsbury, and Erika Wilde

Discover the Lexi Blake Crossover Collection

Available now!

CLOSE COVER by Lexi Blake

Remy Guidry doesn't do relationships. He tried the marriage thing once, back in Louisiana, and learned the hard way that all he really needs in life is a cold beer, some good friends, and the occasional hookup. His job as a bodyguard with McKay-Taggart gives him purpose and lovely perks, like access to Sanctum. The last thing he needs in his life is a woman with stars in her eyes and babies in her future.

Lisa Daley's life is going in the right direction. She has graduated from college after years of putting herself through school. She's got a new job at an accounting firm and she's finished her Sanctum training. Finally on her own and having fun, her life seems pretty perfect. Except she's lonely and the one man she wants won't give her a second look.

There is one other little glitch. Apparently, her new firm is really a front for the mob and now they want her dead. Assassins can really ruin a fun girls' night out. Suddenly strapped to the very same six-foot-five-inch hunk of a bodyguard who makes her heart pound, Lisa can't decide if this situation is a blessing or a curse.

As the mob closes in, Remy takes his tempting new charge back to the safest place he knows—his home in the bayou. Surrounded by his past, he can't help wondering if Lisa is his future. To answer that question, he just has to keep her alive.

* * * *

HER GUARDIAN ANGEL by Larissa Ione

After a difficult childhood and a turbulent stint in the military, Declan Burke finally got his act together. Now he's a battle-hardened professional bodyguard who takes his job at McKay-Taggart seriously and his playtime – and his play*mates* – just as seriously. One thing he never does, however, is mix business with pleasure. But when the mysterious, gorgeous Suzanne D'Angelo needs his protection from a stalker, his desire for her burns out of control, tempting him to break all the rules…even as he's drawn into a dark, dangerous world he didn't know existed.

Suzanne is an earthbound angel on her critical first mission: protecting Declan from an emerging supernatural threat at all costs. To keep him close, she hires him as her bodyguard. It doesn't take long for her to realize that she's in over her head, defenseless against this devastatingly sexy human who makes her crave his forbidden touch.

Together they'll have to draw on every ounce of their collective training to resist each other as the enemy closes in, but soon it becomes apparent that nothing could have prepared them for the menace to their lives…or their hearts.

* * * *

JUSTIFY ME by J. Kenner

McKay-Taggart operative Riley Blade has no intention of returning to Los Angeles after his brief stint as a consultant on mega-star Lyle Tarpin's latest action flick. Not even for Natasha Black, Tarpin's sexy personal assistant who'd gotten under his skin. Why would he, when Tasha made it absolutely clear that—attraction or not—she wasn't interested in a fling, much less a relationship.

But when Riley learns that someone is stalking her, he races to her side. Determined to not only protect her, but to convince her that—no matter what has hurt her in the past—he's not only going to fight for her, he's going to win her heart. Forever.

* * * *

SAY YOU WON'T LET GO by Corinne Michaels

I've had two goals my entire life:

1. Make it big in country music.
2. Get the hell out of Bell Buckle.

I was doing it. I was on my way, until Cooper Townsend landed backstage at my show in Dallas.

This gorgeous, rugged, man of few words was one cowboy I couldn't afford to let distract me. But with his slow smile and rough hands, I just couldn't keep away.

Now, there are outside forces conspiring against us. Maybe we should've known better? Maybe not. Even with the protection from Wade Rycroft, bodyguard for McKay-Taggart, I still don't feel safe. I won't let him get hurt because of me. All I know is that I want to hold on, but know the right thing to do is to let go…

* * * *

HIS TO PROTECT by Carly Phillips

Talia Shaw has spent her adult life working as a scientist for a big pharmaceutical company. She's focused on saving lives, not living life. When her lab is broken into and it's clear someone is after the top secret formula she's working on, she turns to the one man she can trust. The same irresistible man she turned away years earlier because she was too young and naive to believe a sexy guy like Shane Landon could want *her*.

Shane Landon's bodyguard work for McKay-Taggart is the one thing that brings him satisfaction in his life. Relationships come in second to the job. Always. Then little brainiac Talia Shaw shows up in his backyard, frightened and on the run, and his world is turned upside down. And not just because she's found him naked in his outdoor shower, either.

With Talia's life in danger, Shane has to get her out of town and to her eccentric, hermit mentor who has the final piece of the formula she's been working on, while keeping her safe from the men who are after her. Guarding Talia's body certainly isn't any hardship, but he never expects to fall hard and fast for his best friend's little sister and the only woman who's ever really gotten under his skin.

* * * *

RESCUING SADIE by Susan Stoker

Sadie Jennings was used to being protected. As the niece of Sean Taggart, and the receptionist at McKay-Taggart Group, she was constantly surrounded by Alpha men more than capable, and willing, to lay down their life for her. But when she visits her friend in San Antonio, and acts on suspicious activity at Milena's workplace, Sadie puts both of them in the crosshairs of a madman. After several harrowing weeks, her friend is now safe, but for Sadie, the repercussions of her rash act linger on.

Chase Jackson, no stranger to dangerous situations as a captain in the US Army, has volunteered himself as Sadie's bodyguard. He fell head over heels for the beautiful woman the first time he laid eyes on her. With a Delta Force team at his back, he reassures the Taggart's that Sadie will be safe. But when the situation in San Antonio catches up with her, Chase has to use everything he's learned over his career to keep his promise...and to keep Sadie alive long enough to officially make her his.

Discover 1001 Dark Nights Collection Five

Go to www.1001DarkNights.com for more information.

BLAZE ERUPTING by Rebecca Zanetti
Scorpius Syndrome/A Brigade Novella

ROUGH RIDE by Kristen Ashley
A Chaos Novella

HAWKYN by Larissa Ione
A Demonica Underworld Novella

RIDE DIRTY by Laura Kaye
A Raven Riders Novella

ROME'S CHANCE by Joanna Wylde
A Reapers MC Novella

THE MARRIAGE ARRANGEMENT by Jennifer Probst
A Marriage to a Billionaire Novella

SURRENDER by Elisabeth Naughton
A House of Sin Novella

INKED NIGHT by Carrie Ann Ryan
A Montgomery Ink Novella

ENVY by Rachel Van Dyken
An Eagle Elite Novella

PROTECTED by Lexi Blake
A Masters and Mercenaries Novella

THE PRINCE by Jennifer L. Armentrout
A Wicked Novella

PLEASE ME by J. Kenner
A Stark Ever After Novella

WOUND TIGHT by Lorelei James
A Rough Riders/Blacktop Cowboys Novella®

STRONG by Kylie Scott
A Stage Dive Novella

DRAGON NIGHT by Donna Grant
A Dark Kings Novella

TEMPTING BROOKE by Kristen Proby
A Big Sky Novella

HAUNTED BE THE HOLIDAYS by Heather Graham
A Krewe of Hunters Novella

CONTROL by K. Bromberg
An Everyday Heroes Novella

HUNKY HEARTBREAKER by Kendall Ryan
A Whiskey Kisses Novella

THE DARKEST CAPTIVE by Gena Showalter
A Lords of the Underworld Novella

Discover 1001 Dark Nights Collection One

Go to www.1001DarkNights.com for more information.

FOREVER WICKED by Shayla Black
CRIMSON TWILIGHT by Heather Graham
CAPTURED IN SURRENDER by Liliana Hart
SILENT BITE: A SCANGUARDS WEDDING by Tina Folsom
DUNGEON GAMES by Lexi Blake
AZAGOTH by Larissa Ione
NEED YOU NOW by Lisa Renee Jones
SHOW ME, BABY by Cherise Sinclair
ROPED IN by Lorelei James
TEMPTED BY MIDNIGHT by Lara Adrian
THE FLAME by Christopher Rice
CARESS OF DARKNESS by Julie Kenner

Also from 1001 Dark Nights

TAME ME by J. Kenner

Discover 1001 Dark Nights Collection Two

Go to www.1001DarkNights.com for more information.

WICKED WOLF by Carrie Ann Ryan
WHEN IRISH EYES ARE HAUNTING by Heather Graham
EASY WITH YOU by Kristen Proby
MASTER OF FREEDOM by Cherise Sinclair
CARESS OF PLEASURE by Julie Kenner
ADORED by Lexi Blake
HADES by Larissa Ione
RAVAGED by Elisabeth Naughton
DREAM OF YOU by Jennifer L. Armentrout
STRIPPED DOWN by Lorelei James
RAGE/KILLIAN by Alexandra Ivy/Laura Wright
DRAGON KING by Donna Grant
PURE WICKED by Shayla Black
HARD AS STEEL by Laura Kaye
STROKE OF MIDNIGHT by Lara Adrian
ALL HALLOWS EVE by Heather Graham
KISS THE FLAME by Christopher Rice
DARING HER LOVE by Melissa Foster
TEASED by Rebecca Zanetti
THE PROMISE OF SURRENDER by Liliana Hart

Also from 1001 Dark Nights

THE SURRENDER GATE By Christopher Rice
SERVICING THE TARGET By Cherise Sinclair

Discover 1001 Dark Nights Collection Three

Go to www.1001DarkNights.com for more information.

HIDDEN INK by Carrie Ann Ryan
BLOOD ON THE BAYOU by Heather Graham
SEARCHING FOR MINE by Jennifer Probst
DANCE OF DESIRE by Christopher Rice
ROUGH RHYTHM by Tessa Bailey
DEVOTED by Lexi Blake
Z by Larissa Ione
FALLING UNDER YOU by Laurelin Paige
EASY FOR KEEPS by Kristen Proby
UNCHAINED by Elisabeth Naughton
HARD TO SERVE by Laura Kaye
DRAGON FEVER by Donna Grant
KAYDEN/SIMON by Alexandra Ivy/Laura Wright
STRUNG UP by Lorelei James
MIDNIGHT UNTAMED by Lara Adrian
TRICKED by Rebecca Zanetti
DIRTY WICKED by Shayla Black
THE ONLY ONE by Lauren Blakely
SWEET SURRENDER by Liliana Hart

Discover 1001 Dark Nights Collection Four

Go to www.1001DarkNights.com for more information.

ROCK CHICK REAWAKENING by Kristen Ashley
ADORING INK by Carrie Ann Ryan
SWEET RIVALRY by K. Bromberg
SHADE'S LADY by Joanna Wylde
RAZR by Larissa Ione
ARRANGED by Lexi Blake
TANGLED by Rebecca Zanetti
HOLD ME by J. Kenner
SOMEHOW, SOME WAY by Jennifer Probst
TOO CLOSE TO CALL by Tessa Bailey
HUNTED by Elisabeth Naughton
EYES ON YOU by Laura Kaye
BLADE by Alexandra Ivy/Laura Wright
DRAGON BURN by Donna Grant
TRIPPED OUT by Lorelei James
STUD FINDER by Lauren Blakely
MIDNIGHT UNLEASHED by Lara Adrian
HALLOW BE THE HAUNT by Heather Graham
DIRTY FILTHY FIX by Laurelin Paige
THE BED MATE by Kendall Ryan
PRINCE ROMAN by CD Reiss
NO RESERVATIONS by Kristen Proby
DAWN OF SURRENDER by Liliana Hart

Also from 1001 Dark Nights

TEMPT ME by J. Kenner

About Lexi Blake

Lexi Blake lives in North Texas with her husband, three kids, and the laziest rescue dog in the world. She began writing at a young age, concentrating on plays and journalism. It wasn't until she started writing romance that she found success. She likes to find humor in the strangest places. Lexi believes in happy endings no matter how odd the couple, threesome or foursome may seem. She also writes contemporary Western ménage as Sophie Oak.

Connect with Lexi online:

Facebook: Lexi Blake
Twitter: authorlexiblake
Website: www.LexiBlake.net

Discover More Lexi Blake

Arranged: A Masters and Mercenaries Novella by Lexi Blake, Now Available

Kash Kamdar is the king of a peaceful but powerful island nation. As Loa Mali's sovereign, he is always in control, the final authority. Until his mother uses an ancient law to force her son into marriage. His prospective queen is a buttoned-up intellectual, nothing like Kash's usual party girl. Still, from the moment of their forced engagement, he can't stop thinking about her.

Dayita Samar comes from one of Loa Mali's most respected families. The Oxford-educated scientist has dedicated her life to her country's future. But under her staid and calm exterior, Day hides a few sexy secrets of her own. She is willing to marry her king, but also agrees that they can circumvent the law. Just because they're married doesn't mean they have to change their lives. It certainly doesn't mean they have to fall in love.

After one wild weekend in Dallas, Kash discovers his bride-to-be is more than she seems. Engulfed in a changing world, Kash finds exciting new possibilities for himself. Could Day help him find respite from the crushing responsibility he's carried all his life? This fairy tale could have a happy ending, if only they can escape Kash's past…

* * * *

Dungeon Games: A Masters and Mercenaries Novella by Lexi Blake, Now Available

Obsessed

Derek Brighton has become one of Dallas's finest detectives through a combination of discipline and obsession. Once he has a target in his sights, nothing can stop him. When he isn't solving homicides, he applies the same intensity to his playtime at Sanctum, a secretive BDSM club. Unfortunately, no amount of beautiful submissives can fill the hole that one woman left in his heart.

Unhinged

Karina Mills has a reputation for being reckless, and her clients appreciate her results. As a private investigator, she pursues her cases with nothing holding her back. In her personal life, Karina yearns for something different. Playing at Sanctum has been a safe way to find peace, but the one Dom who could truly master her heart is out of reach.

Enflamed

On the hunt for a killer, Derek enters a shadowy underworld only to find the woman he aches for is working the same case. Karina is searching for a missing girl and won't stop until she finds her. To get close to their prime suspect, they need to pose as a couple. But as their operation goes under the covers, unlikely partners become passionate lovers while the killer prepares to strike.

* * * *

Adored: A Masters and Mercenaries Novella by Lexi Blake, Now Available

A man who gave up on love

Mitch Bradford is an intimidating man. In his professional life, he has a reputation for demolishing his opponents in the courtroom. At the exclusive BDSM club Sanctum, he prefers disciplining pretty submissives with no strings attached. In his line of work, there's no time for a healthy relationship. After a few failed attempts, he knows he's not good for any woman—especially not his best friend's sister.

A woman who always gets what she wants

Laurel Daley knows what she wants, and her sights are set on Mitch. He's smart and sexy, and it doesn't matter that he's a few years older and has a couple of bitter ex-wives. Watching him in action at work and at play, she knows he just needs a little polish to make some woman the perfect lover. She intends to be that woman, but first she has to show him how good it could be.

A killer lurking in the shadows

When an unexpected turn of events throws the two together, Mitch and Laurel are confronted with the perfect opportunity to explore their mutual desire. Night after night of being close breaks down Mitch's defenses. The more he sees of Laurel, the more he knows he wants her. Unfortunately, someone else has their eyes on Laurel and they have murder in mind.

* * * *

Devoted: A Masters and Mercenaries Novella by Lexi Blake, Now Available

A woman's work

Amy Slaten has devoted her life to Slaten Industries. After ousting her corrupt father and taking over the CEO role, she thought she could relax and enjoy taking her company to the next level. But an old business rivalry rears its ugly head. The only thing that can possibly take her mind off business is the training class at Sanctum…and her training partner, the gorgeous and funny Flynn Adler. If she can just manage to best her mysterious business rival, life might be perfect.

A man's commitment

Flynn Adler never thought he would fall for the enemy. Business is war, or so his father always claimed. He was raised to be ruthless when it came to the family company, and now he's raising his brother to one day work with him. The first order of business? The hostile takeover of Slaten Industries. It's a stressful job so when his brother offers him a spot in Sanctum's training program, Flynn jumps at the chance.

A lifetime of devotion….

When Flynn realizes the woman he's falling for is none other than the CEO of the firm he needs to take down, he has to make a choice. Does he take care of the woman he's falling in love with or the business he's worked a lifetime to build? And when Amy finally understands the man she's come to trust is none other than the enemy, will she walk away from him or fight for the love she's come to depend on?

Memento Mori

Masters and Mercenaries: The Forgotten, Book 1
By Lexi Blake
Coming August 28, 2018

Six men with no memories of the past
One leader with no hope for the future

A man without a past

Jax woke up in a lab, his memories erased, and his mind reprogrammed to serve a mad woman's will. After being liberated from his prison, he pledged himself to the only thing he truly knows—his team. Six men who lost everything they were. They must make certain no one else gets their hands on the drugs that stole their lives, all while hiding from every intelligence organization on the planet. The trail has led him to an unforgiving mountainside and a beautiful wilderness expert who may be his only hope of finding the truth.

A woman with a bright future

River Lee knows her way around the Colorado wilderness. She's finally found a home in a place called Bliss after years lost in darkness. The nature guide prefers to show her clients the beauty found in the land, but she also knows the secrets the mountains hold. When she meets Jax, something about the troubled man calls to her. She agrees to lead him to the site of an abandoned government facility hidden deep in the forest. She never dreamed she was stepping into the middle of a battlefield.

A love that could heal a broken soul

Spending time with River, Jax discovers a peace he's never known. Their passion unlocks a side of himself he didn't even know he was missing. When an old enemy makes his first move, Jax and River find themselves fighting for their lives. But when his past is revealed, will River be caught in the crosshairs of a global conspiracy?

* * * *

"The mens at bar asked me to send this to you." Alexei placed a massive mound of cheese fries in front of them. "I tell them most mens send women drinks, but they use word *consent* very much."

River laughed, really laughed for the first time in forever. It was good to know Me Too had hit southern Colorado. They'd sent cheese fries as their lure to catch a date for the evening.

Heather's eyes were practically glowing in the dim light. "There's no way we can eat all of this."

"I think they were counting on it," she replied. She wasn't ready for this. But when would she be? If she never got back out there, Matt won. When she thought about it, not dating was akin to letting the terrorists win.

Not that it would be a date. It would be a lot of watching the hottest man she'd ever met hit on her friend. She hoped Hottie's friend was fun to talk to.

"Alexei, could you invite them over?" She was going to be brave, if only for her friend's sake.

The big Russian walked off and it wasn't more than a minute before they were standing at the booth.

He took her breath away. She glanced down at his feet. Sneakers, but they weren't the flashy kind worn to show off how much cash a man had. These were well worn, subtle. They were working shoes, like the jeans he wore. Nothing ripped or torn and yet she could tell he'd worn them down to soft denim.

"Hello. I'm Jax." His voice was deep but there was a musical quality to it. She would bet he could sing. "This is my brother, Tucker."

Brothers. They oddly didn't look a lot alike, but she'd seen siblings who she would never have guessed came from the same parents. Tucker wasn't bad himself. Dark, wavy hair any woman would love to have. It was slightly overgrown but did nothing but enhance his male-model beauty. He seemed far softer than his incredibly masculine friend.

Her first impression of Jax hadn't been false. He was broad and muscular, his face defined by stark planes and lines. He looked predatory and hungry.

She could barely breath. Maybe this was a mistake. She would have a hard time watching this gorgeous man fawn all over Heather.

Something about him pulled her in, made her want to forget that she had terrible taste in men. It was like there was some invisible tether connecting her to him.

Except that was stupid because he couldn't be here for her.

"I'm Heather and my very quiet friend's name is River." Heather was smiling that ridiculously sunny smile of hers, the one no man could resist. "Thanks for the fries. You know normally men send over drinks. I'm glad you're so concerned with consent. That's very forward thinking of you."

Tucker shook his head. "We're not allowed to have sex without consent. Do we need a note? Like a contract?"

Jax jabbed an elbow in his brother's ribs. "He's being a weirdo and moving way, way too fast. Sorry about that. He doesn't get out much."

Tucker frowned and said something under his breath that sounded like *neither do you*, but then a sweet smile came over his face. "Sorry. Sometimes my jokes fall flat. Can we please join you? We're in town for a week or so and besides the Russian dude, we haven't met anyone."

"Sure." Heather slid over.

River did the same, expecting Tucker to slide in next to her, but it was Jax's big body that moved beside her. She felt tiny compared to him. She watched as Heather grinned her way as though to say *you were wrong*.

Tucker sat beside Heather and started passing out the small plates.

Jax probably wanted to be able to look at Heather. That was it.

God, he smelled good. She kind of wanted to lean over and run her nose along his shoulder and up his neck. He smelled like soap and sandalwood.

"Can I get you some? I like French fries but they're even better with cheese and bacon. I think maybe everything is better with cheese and bacon, but if you want something else, I'll get it for you. You can have anything on the menu. And I'll buy the wine or beer or whatever. I merely wanted you to understand I don't want to get drunk tonight. I would rather get to know you."

She turned, expecting to see Jax staring across at Heather. Nope. Those stunning green eyes were staring at her expectantly. He had a plate in his hand as though waiting for her permission to serve her.

Her. He was looking at her.

"She does talk," Heather said. "I've heard her and everything."

"Yeah, I would love some." She was hungry, actually. It was odd. Her stomach kind of rumbled, but in a good way. For the last year and a half it seemed she'd lost her appetite and had to force herself to eat, but tonight she smelled the fries and cheese and bacon and wanted.

And she wanted him, too. She wasn't going to lie to herself. This time she would be smart. If he turned out to be a nice guy, she might spend the night with him. Might. And then she would send him on his way because he was a tourist.

She wouldn't fall for him because she wouldn't spend more than a night.

On behalf of 1001 Dark Nights,

Liz Berry and M.J. Rose would like to thank ~

Steve Berry
Doug Scofield
Kim Guidroz
Jillian Stein
InkSlinger PR
Dan Slater
Asha Hossain
Chris Graham
Fedora Chen
Kasi Alexander
Jessica Johns
Dylan Stockton
Richard Blake
and Simon Lipskar

Made in the USA
Middletown, DE
27 August 2018